THE LODGERS

Also by Holly Pester

POETRY

Comic Timing

The Lodgers

Holly Pester

Assembly Press
Prince Edward County, Ontario

First published in Great Britain by Granta Books, 2024

Library and Archives Canada Cataloguing in Publication

Title: The lodgers / Holly Pester.

Names: Pester, Holly, author.

Description: Previously published: London: Granta Books, 2024.

Identifiers: Canadiana (print) 20240407377 | Canadiana (ebook) 20240409396 | ISBN 9781738009862 (softcover) | ISBN 9781738009879 (EPUB)

Subjects: LCGFT: Novels.

Classification: LCC PR6116.E88 L63 2024 | DDC 823/.92—dc23

Printed and bound in Canada

Typeset in Adobe Jenson Pro
Cover design © Jo Walker

Assembly Press
assemblypress.ca

THE LODGERS

Moffa the Town

As a bored and nervous young girl I often imagined climbing inside a small case or container, like a piano stool or matchbox, a washing-machine drum or bread bin, and living in there. The soft foam bed at the bottom of a box of earring studs was arousing. I liked tool boxes with compartments, half-empty tubs of cotton buds, or miniature drawers, even car boots. For the fantasy to work, they had to be containers with strong interiors. A ledge of any kind got me going. I'd get excited by shapes that resembled steps. I could stare into little spaces for hours, feeling my body wishing itself transported into the tiny dwelling, not to be happy but to be hidden, packed away and secretly private, having a pretend little life. The open-plan kitchen and living room of my subletter's flat reminded me of those spaces.

Now full of my bags, the room, already architecturally odd for the sake of marketable style, was chaotic. An absurdly awkward corner shape, its most extreme point was above a chugging boiler to the right of the sink. All the sides and optimism of the flat met there to disappear. I stared into the corner's centre with parched, gritty eyes and felt sucked towards it. I had been travelling all day. Early-September sun flickering through the train windows had given me a strange head. Nothing felt real. What had I arrived at? The flat was arranged around a kitchenette and counter, a staffroomish table and chairs on the other side of that, a two-seater Argos sofa, a black MDF TV stand where there might once have been a TV but not now, not for me. Buy-to-let laminate flooring throughout. The flat was compact and hot and, like a lot of short-term adult accommodation, kitted out by small acts of shopping for low-cost utensils, designed to be nice enough but not to last long, like fat yellow cutlery that falls to pieces. The flat smelt of men's shower gel and repeated nights of instant noodles. It was hard to do anything except linger with the odours, the actions of travel still churning in me. My mind wouldn't settle, believing there was more journey to do.

There was too much to think about on the go, too many timetables and gestures to condition my thinking. Hauling myself up steps and over gaps, whipping tickets through slots, excusing my feet, minding clumsy people, whacking my increasing accumulation of bags on barriers, sweating on seats and smiling when it made sense to—all the time, my instincts hooked to directions. I felt nervous then sleepy, nervous then sleepy on and off all day. When I finally arrived at my destination—a '90s new-build block of flats called Mills Hope Gardens adjacent to the high street of a small market town—I had to get on my knees and find a pretend rock near a bush, then wriggle a set of keys from inside it. I heard myself breathe heavily on the stairwell, all the while keeping hold of my bags, and lurched through a number of doors before reaching the last one, finally dropping my bags upon the sudden need to pee, squeezing it in and finding the bathroom that whirred when I switched the light on, saw myself in the mirror and that I was still a tired woman of train stations, rubbed my dry skin, sat on the toilet and sent a message saying, I'm in! When I came back from the bathroom my bags looked sad. They had been so heavy to carry, but when set down amounted to hardly anything at all—just a holdall, a rucksack and some canvas sacks, now deflated like invalid lambs. It made me feel stupid. If only it was only my armpits that cried. You would cry if you were my armpit, straining under that rubbish all day. Who was I afterwards? I had journeyed; had been myself in transit. I waited on concourses under difficult lights, squinted, put my coffee down on the floor between my feet and stared up at information. I flowed along the arbitrary lines of a route until my toes stung, then walked, semi-gallantly, into this building, then into this flat. Now who was I? Stood in some man-smell but still myself in transit. I wasn't used to it. It's hard to get used to the feeling of arriving somewhere I will live in but don't yet understand, to know it will soon feel natural here but for now feels corpse-like. I aspired to this homely feeling, so paced around in the smell, and, being someone who can't take their coat off, sat down to speed-read the contract left out for me on a table and cross-check an inventory which included a stain.

On one side of the flat was a pair of long, narrow windows with nice deep sills, on the other side there were three heavy doors in a row, one to the bathroom, the next for my bedroom. I went inside my bedroom, it was as featureless as a till receipt, but it would do. The bed was 'small double' or a 'large single,' depending on your outlook, there was a cheap white chest of drawers with the bottom drawer a little wonky, and next to that a wardrobe made of calico. I exited my bedroom spiritless. The final door was marked with a Post-it note saying 'Kav's Room.' It had been suggested in my irregular communications with my young subletter that *someone else* would be in the flat at *some point,* but I'd imagined that someone being far away from me, down a long corridor. The smallness of the actual flat and location of the bedroom door adjacent to what was now my bedroom door made me less happy, less relaxed about Kav. Kav whose threatened presence now pertained to a person and a door that I would hear. When will Kav come? I pushed open Kav's door and peeked into the room. It was blacked out by blinds. I shut the door quickly. Why was I so jumpy about the idea of a person? I'll meet Kav and have business-friendly conversations about the heating or the post, or some other imperative of new roommates. The bedroom next to Kav's was mine and that would have to be OK. I opened and immediately closed Kav's door again. Kav could walk in at any minute.

I sat at the table pierced by a vinegary sunshine and got out the sandwich I had been carrying with me since that morning, set it down with the contract. The sandwich was one of the only vegetarian options at the train station shop, and was still in the box, hardening and weeping humous. For some reason I ate it, I wasn't happy. But as a result the triangular box was empty, with an inside that resembled, like sarcasm, the one I was in. I looked inside. It had a window too. It was me who brought the sandwich here, it was my demonstration. So I put the empty box on the nice deep windowsill. The bin yet to be found.

Anything less than an hour felt too soon to unpack so I sat at the table, looking at the contract I had just signed. How pathetic it all was. My signature like a child's pretending to be grown-up had me promising to be accountable for rent, agreeing to not not pay it, and to guard the very basic features of the flat from damage. Some of the instructions felt copied from generic contracts, others were typed in the subletter's own voice: pay the rent into this bank account, but don't say rent on the reference, say *birthday money* or something. Don't say who you are to neighbours. Don't let the smoke alarms go off. Use the extractor. Don't fry bacon and forget. Be very quiet. A paranoid boy had written the contract not knowing whether he did or did not want this arrangement to be official. Ultimately it was for his peace of mind, and mine, and Kav's—if Kav had a mind. I signed it: I hereby agree that you are a paranoid boy. For this boy, my subletter, the contract was a foil for his sudden and suspicious departure. For me, the contract said one thing and one thing only, it said the same thing as the sandwich box and the pretend rock, the same thing as the keys going into the door and turning. What it said to me was that I was here again, I was back, back from the great nowhere of somewhere else, returned, all too actually, to the whereabouts of Moffa.

* * *

My phone buzzed with a message, Ur in! Followed by, Is Kav there? No! I replied, then: When will he be here? There was no response until, Hope all OK! Will be off my phone for a few weeks. Bins Thurs. I waited for more messages but there were none. That was the end of the conversation.

I got up and checked the view from the long, narrow windows. They were on the wrong side, all I could see was the back of a balti restaurant and some car park. I went into my bedroom and stood on the bed's bare mattress with my shoes on. There it was, Moffa's house. A telling corner of it at the end of a street of small terraced houses. There you are, I said aloud and imagined her in there, gliding from room to room conveying cut flowers and coughing. My arms lifted like wings as I stretched my neck to see the sun setting on the roof that covered her, a lid on her uncontrollable voice. I jumped off the bed and stood even more cluelessly in the main room. The smell was no longer noticeable. It was no longer a new flat. It was where I lived, I was back.

One year ago today I made a different journey and arrived somewhere else, at another small town in this same country under last year's early-September sun. It was a similarly proportioned town, closer to the coast but still the sort of place where cars slowly communicate along roads like big dumb foreheads, and there's a market on Thursdays, and a small funded museum for no good reason. I stayed there for some time, half a year, and then left. The situation was odd, or maybe so normal that I couldn't help making it complicated. I think that's what most living set-ups are: you take a very banal arrangement involving someone paying to live somewhere where other people also live (or at least one other person), and without anything much happening, the whole thing becomes furiously operatic. I'd say it takes a couple of weeks for things to unravel, and then reconnect hyperactively. Bodies do what they do and the rent can only make it so rational. I stayed in that town near to the coast for the agreed six months, and then left. No goodbyes. A new woman is arriving there now. That's probably true. Today is just the sort of day people arrive at new and knotty tenancies. Her suitcase is trundling along the pavement.

She must be a little like me, she made the same decisions based on the same limited options, and now she's there. I like to imagine how she is feeling and compare it to how I felt. I like to compare. How else can we do this? I wouldn't get out of the bath if I couldn't imagine other people doing it. I wouldn't do anything. My life is a triangle of where I am, have been and want to be; of what I crave, don't have and can't have; of who I miss, hate ... forget. In the new flat I was tired and un-unpacked. I sat down, still in my coat, on the cola-stained sofa, got comfy, hated it, and set to work imagining you.

You arrive

September is when people arrive, and you're there now, in a different town, walking towards an address that I arrived at one year ago. You have heavy bags. You are younger, summer is nearly over. You walk slower than me, with a stone in your shoe, a strap mark on your arm. There are pineapples on your socks, your thin coat is off and hanging over your wheelie case, nearly dragging on the floor, you're taller and have longer limbs that can be awkward if you don't stand up straight, but pretty elegant when you do. It depends how you feel in the situation you're in. Today you're nervous because you're starting something new, a big life change, that you yourself have instigated. The world turns, people are churned out and flop onto their next phase of life. There's nothing terribly interesting in that, a room in a house is let and let again, but I'm fixated with the fact; the order of me, then you, in the same room. I know precisely the arrangements that led you down the street you are walking along. To the house you are approaching. They were the same as mine, I went there. I was like you. And so you might have a feeling you know me too. You're feeling it now as you walk with the edge of your body facing its plan. Maybe you also have a way of trying to return to an idea of homeliness that hurts and heals, and involves a lot of train travel. Maybe you also shift debt around and email strangers, and move through life trying to be in the right place but keep ending up in slightly the wrong place. You're looking for something—no, actually, you're hoping that some glorious alternative is looking for you. You've been making yourself available to it in all sorts of places and people until today, when you will plant your readiness in someone else's house. Your route is one I've taken before, it ends on the riposte of a cul-de-sac. You walk the directions and count the house numbers just like I did. Parked outside one house is a taxi, outside another is a small boat. The houses are identical in shape but with small giveaways about the occupiers' financial ups and downs: a loft conversion, a conservatory, peeling paint, a broken slat in the blinds. They all have cars. Finally, there you are in front of a house I know well, repeating my circumstance, standing on the same spot in different shoes. The house is loved, I remember feeling that, o, a real mother lives here. A warmth, a floral smell, a careful zoning of safety and cheer, its work well-hidden, I felt it. Do you notice? I don't think you do.

And yet, you came here. You're moving in. How do you like the house? How do you like its 1970s eaves, its wide tiled roof under the quiet residential sky? The early-autumn heat makes the concrete drive sparkle ready for you, it tips you to a small step up to the door. To the side is a petal-shaped plate of cat food for a cat that refuses to come inside. I remember kicking the cat food but you miss it, you're already a more careful iteration, moving with the intention of a map. The house looms at you loaded, you've come at it empty. You're arriving like I did—as an animated decision. You have made it to this house that looks like the set of insurance adverts that, years from now, will be the setting for a dream you keep having. Try not to think past the first night, simply ring the doorbell and hold your face ready. You notice you're early, press the bell sensing you've disrupted the house's inside. You hear noises, then see through the bumpy glass of the front door that there is a child on the other side. Her aspect smudges upwards until the shape of her face resembles a giant wasp's. A woman's voice calls, Coming! but it is the child who opens the door, then holds it half-open, greeting you and rejecting you at the same time with a frown. The girl is about as tall as a Hoover or a swan, she has a tough, tiny body and a otterish face, full of questions and puzzles. Behind her the mother is telling her to move out of the way and let you in. The girl opens the door just enough for you to funnel through the vestibule and into the living room, into their life and its blessed centre.

The child is excited. She looks at every bit of you and your belongings like they're something for her. Does she still wear a uniform the colour of mud and lemons? It clashes with the silver carpet she leaps around on, circling a mess of school bags, shouting, Hello hell-ow hell-owuh stranger. Clearly and immediately she is what controls the moods of the house, including the dog that growls at you from the sofa, backing up from its sleep. I remember asking the child's name and tilting my neck to her. You ask her also. She shouts her name back to you to an improvised tune as she flings her hair from side to side so you have to ask her to say it again. Instead of answering, this time she runs into the sofa with a bump, wraps her arms around the dog, pivots back to you to steal the chocolate from your bag. And with that transaction you cross over into her life, a life that fans outwards in invisible ribbons that strangle and embellish everything. A dog toy thunks onto the floor, I wouldn't have touched it but you do. The dog is bigger now but still nervous of strangers. The girl looks confused by your presence, and also cross with you, and also excited, but accepts that you have a name, a name she shall squawk in an hour from her bath. You say something like, I am pleased to meet you. She laughs and shouts, No! After that she ignores your small questions and instead describes the rules around shoes: You have to take them off and throw them in the bin. She states with authority that this is: A house without men, we have to lock them in the toilet if they come here, Mummy has to kill them and you have to help. She says you have to sleep in Mummy's *beauty puh-ar-lour*. The word 'parlour' wells from her mouth in three parts, signalling the room's importance and your privilege in being allowed to sleep there. Nodding and smiling, you say you'll sleep in any room you're told to, you'll go there now and with the mug of tea you've been handed and put it on the windowsill.

Once you're in your single room, a room that feels too small to be a parlour, you go to the window and look across the cul-de-sac. You acknowledge the cars poised in their drives forewarning the morning. You acknowledge the tight squares of green, a single upright tree, two teenage girls walking with linked arms. Then you realise you are being watched. The girl is lingering at your door and giggling. You can come in, you say. She shakes her head. This is all new to you. She runs in and jumps on the bed. OK then, you say, unsure how to manage children and nervous especially of this one. She jumps three times then runs out, leaving a folded-up note like a rabbit leaving droppings. The note is a welcome card for you, it has an attempt at your name in pen across a crayon drawing of the sun. Inside it says, 'don't be like Joe.' You find out later that Joe is a classmate she despises.

* * *

The economy of you entering that house for the first time, as I once did, is as specific as baking: the transactions, the equivalents, the values that are substance, the values that are pressure, the timing and the work and the promises, the heat, the shape, the terms. A single night costs £27. Five nights per week is £130 and you can add Saturday and Sunday nights if you need, and it is assumed that you won't. The £27 covers a room from between the hours of 6 p.m. and 9 a.m. as well as: a choice of cereal, a choice of milk, a choice of white or brown sliced bread for toast, a choice of tea or coffee, a sachet of instant hot chocolate for the evening, unlimited biscuits from the purple tin, ordinary soap and shower gel, clean, dry towels and bedding, beds made, vacuumed bedroom floors, a clean bathroom, a clean downstairs toilet and shower room, toilet-roll replenishment, breakfast items washed up, basic condiments, salt and pepper, the use of pots and pans for cooking an evening meal (which must be tidied up completely for the morning), a newly cut front-door key and keyring, your share of energy and water bills, use of Wi-Fi, access to the TV occasionally, access to the fruit bowl, occasionally, if there is enough fruit. The day's costings are agreed. The arrangements are agreed. The price is over what you budgeted for but it's so nice here, with them and the warm sweetness of a family semi. (The only other place you've seen was a damp house share with three PhD students—men from southern counties in their twenties—and when you went to be interviewed by them they were all eating kebabs, playing video games, listening to Bach and … swaying?) You have decided to treat yourself to some homeliness, the most expensive of things, and trust your loan will cover the first few months. You're building something up that will be released and returned to later. Life matter will steam and breathe its air back in your face when you're done. You're also providing. There are things that are now in the fridge—gassy and long-lasting or cheesy and fresh—because you came here. I was also part of the produce. Maybe you'll drink milk that I paid for. Everyone needs to eat. Everyone is paying for someone to. Nothing is as direct as eggs and there's nothing direct about bread.

* * *

You are hot. You have roughly unpacked your pyjamas and washbag and are sitting back downstairs on the pink sofa. It is without many points of reference at all, a warm house. The heat works into you making your neck damp but at the same time it settles you. Your coat has disappeared and you're sitting next to the grumbling dog, like an unwilling shrub, holding a glass of white wine under the glare of the girl whose bedtime teases the conversation you and her mother are trying to have. You mishear the mother and want to be her friend. You catch glimpses of the strength in her arms, her bracelets and hummingbird tattoo, she moves as fast as the girl but with grips instead of sweeps. You hold your conversation over the top of their parent-and-child choreography, making all sorts of predictions about how you'll live with them, how you'll manage your body and habits so they don't clash, telling her that you will go away when you have to but be around if needed, what time you expect to be back every night, that you'd love to share some wine or a beer occasionally, yes, you could help move the trampoline in the garden, you think you can do it next week in time for the last of the nice weather, no, you don't have a bread preference, no bread at all in fact, just muesli, that's what you like, yes, you could sit with her daughter some evenings, yes, everyone needs to get laid, or try to, yes, ha, no, you haven't got a car, or a bike, yes, the room is perfect, no, you haven't heard of the woman who was in it last, yes, it's the same course you're doing, o she sounds nice, o that sounds complicated, yes, it starts tomorrow, yes, you're nervous. The mother goes quiet and looks away often, then returns to the conversation full of smiles. What kind of tea do you drink? she asks, and in the same beat, Are you with someone? They can come over, she says. You say, Just normal tea, thank you, and ignore her other question. She persists, And will anyone be coming over? As she asks this the mother shakes her hair cheekily like her daughter does. You say, No, then you go, Hahah, that's no ... Then you say, I'm single. A minute later she asks the same question again, remembers, then apologises. A distraction keeps hitting her and making her quiet. She works a lot, she doesn't say so outright but in the short conversation you've had so far she's mentioned cleaning houses, dog walking and some accounting for a self-employed neighbour called Ryan who buys and sells motorbike parts and is always trying it on. Ryan, she tuts. All of this work is in addition to the waxing treatments, fringe trims and manicures she does in your bedroom until 6 p.m. most evenings. She is dazzlingly feminine, with the temper of a naturally tireless person who is finally, after years of the daily efforts by others to bring her down, becoming tired.

You and the single mother sit in her living room and make a pact of considerations from what began as an online forum post advertising a single room 'for most of the week' to a 'female possibly mature student or young professional' who must like 'children and gods (dogs),' must be 'quiet and tidy.' You remark on the comfort of the sofa and she makes a sad comment about life not turning out like she thought it would. You move your words to sympathise then realise she means you. You shift in your seat and reimagine yourself as a capable person. You want to help her, she wants to help you. She looks like one of her daughter's dolls, as confidently sexed and as brightly posed. The lines of care and need will get confusing in this house with all these dolls lying around! The girl interrupts the conversation by stroking her mother's hair and lying over her lap. Her skinny back is gently stroked and then tickled. They both laugh in pretty squeaks. You instinctively look away but are thrilled by something in their connection. The girl stands up and leads her mother upstairs by the hand to her bath, leaving you alone on the sofa with the dog. He watches them leave then turns away from you with a grievous sigh. You gulp your wine.

That the child is nothing like how you or I were as children is obvious, little girls have changed since then. They have tougher bones and less fear, they smell sharper and dance more. They are allowed to laugh without covering their mouths. Girls have a new, alert diction, I've noticed, as provoked and as glassy as the world they poke at. But that doesn't stop you wanting to be close to this one. Who knows why? She's considering it too, in her nearly animal brain. As a permitted goodnight the girl returns to you with clean fluffy hair and a thick cotton nightie, hands you another piece of paper as she says quietly, So you can find your way to the toilet, and runs away. What she has handed you is a felt-tip drawing of the house, a cross section of the two floors under a scribbled blue sky and a grinning bird. From the folds it is clear that the drawing has been passed through many hands of invited strangers. Each room is marked by some icon of furniture and a symbol made of two circles with a numbered arrow pointing to them. It says: 'a secrit plan to smak butts.' In the square representing what is now your bedroom there is a pair of buttocks, larger than the door, hovering and charged. You imagine them in your bed, burning hot against the radiator. This is when you first think about me, really, looking at the diagram, it shows that I exist as a name and a story, but also as a body that was in your bed, emanating, spreading forth, tracing sleep curves and having bum cheeks. With outrage and triumph you imagine how yours will go there tonight. I'm sorry, but this rotation of buttocks and welcomes is what you are now economically part of. Get used to it.

* * *

Past midnight you find yourself stepping lightly past the little girl's door on your way to get a glass of water. You stop, feeling and knowing that she's dreaming in her bed with both legs starring out of the duvet. I might have paused on that spot on the landing too, so I could stand in that district of night-time where children sleep. Neither of us have heard it for so long. How different does it feel to sleep in a house with a child in it? What does it do to the night? Where were you last night, for example, were you the surest and clearest one there? I'm asking because I'm trying to picture you and I doubt it.

The mother's door opens and a large angry cat runs out. The mother swears after it but instantly recedes at seeing you. She pulls her T-shirt down to cover herself, apologising, unguarded without make-up or contact lenses, asking sweetly if you are all right, if everything is OK, but she cannot disguise how much she wishes you were not there.

Moffa the bread

My new sublet flat was immaculately childless. I was the only one who needed things here. My thoughts whined, my body got babyish, thirsty and upset, then I'd have to sort myself out. On my way to a tap without the attractive tension of a child sleeping somewhere in the house, I slipped from here to there feeling nothing. A little chill. The glass I found smelt of dirty hair. I rinsed it twice and drank. From the main window the dark back of the high street looked artificial and ill-managed; a small, uninteresting place that loved cars parking without offering much of a reason to drive there. I knew this town too well: the origin point of boredom. Even this new view revealed nothing but an angle that revealed nothing except the stillness of a town at night. How it slouched sedately, leaking light. I am from here, I said to myself, unconvinced, this is my town. The miniature version of the shop sign at the back of the birthday-card shop had been the same since my childhood. Its balloon typography still full of '90s hope and dumb charisma. The bins outside the balti restaurant were full up, with a beer bottle on top.

I heard a noise from somewhere in the building. Someone was returning to their flat in the middle of the night, someone was stomping up the stairs. They were walking along my corridor, they sighed; I suddenly felt very undressed and silly in my leggings and vest with a sleep-shocked face. Kav? Was Kav coming now? I tucked my hair behind my ears, to be ready. I picked up my glass of water, to be natural. I heard a key going into a door—but not this one. The flat opposite mine. Who lived there? Who on earth were they? People who worked late? People who went to the pub and walked back slowly? I decided it was good practice for Kav returning and that next time I should jump back into my bedroom in case it was Kav and we got off to a bad start. No one who returns that late at night wants to be greeted in the dark by a bemused woman. I went back to bed and tried to tune out of the sounds in the building, but the flat was bare and echoey. It needed some cushions and a bookshelf full of books that I no longer had, plus lots of expressive house plants. Maybe Kav would bring plants. Maybe Kav was a kind of plant? I was tired. I tried to picture him properly but could only imagine him based on what I knew of this person so far, which was absolutely nothing except a name and an expectation. What I knew about Kav was that he could appear at any time. Therefore, what I imagined was a creature, specifically a bulbous bin bag with goat legs, that would emerge at night when I wasn't awake and clop about, opening and closing the fridge, grunting, roaming, occupying a liminality, then disappearing into the shadows if I or anything disturbed him. It was a frightening and unnecessary image. Kav was more likely to be a person with a perfectly good reason to be away and would soon have a perfectly good one to come back. It was fine to be alone in the meantime.

I had memories of people passing me a glass of water at night, sensory fragments of a soft arm in the moonlight and another chest breathing. They had to mean that while aloneness is temporary, so is company. Instead of past-people I let myself think about you, and the little girl, and the carpeted landing, as I clicked my knees in my new bed. Cheap sheets. My new bedroom was a long way from the cosy, flowery room of my old lodgings, not at all homely. The white walls were grubby. Someone else's life was packed into boxes under the bed. I didn't like the idea of that. The sad sediment of someone else could waft up and affect my sleep. I couldn't sleep. But it was my first night and nothing to worry about. I put it down to travel buzz and new coordinates. I thought that I might have to move the bed so my head wasn't pointing the wrong way. Perhaps it always would. I tried to relax. My first day was your first day. We both had to deal with our personalities, to answer questions. There would be more questions tomorrow when I walked down that high street in the daytime. I'd have to give more accounts of myself.

* * *

I couldn't sleep. Was someone singing? The beach towel and empty duvet cover I was using as bedding weren't working. I opened some drawers looking for sheets which I had said I'd bring but hadn't. The wonky bottom drawer was so because it was stuffed full of my subletter's ephemera, as I realised when I tried to pull it out and detached the sides from the bottom. Inside, his papers and private notes were disorganised and mingling, a student card, a staff card for a nearby business park, visa correspondence from the government mixed with birthday cards and a pack of playing cards. It was entropic and melancholy except for a loose Polaroid photo of my subletter—a pretty boy or, rather, a young man in his late twenties, with his arm around a similar-looking boy with a shyer face. They had the same tufty bleached hair. I shoved everything back and closed the drawer, got back into bed with a huff. What to think about?

Moffa. Moffa's house. Moffa's house over there. The kitchen, the Charlie Chaplin silhouette clock above the sink. She didn't know I was here yet. What would she have done if she'd known? Would she have baked? No, she wouldn't do that. Moffa tried to make bread once. I remembered walking into the kitchen and finding an abandoned bowl of wet cushiony matter next to some handwritten instructions.

Moffa nowhere. The pen she used must have been running out because the first five instructions were too faint to read and the last one was insanely scratched, INTO THE HOT DO. Maybe she took it as some sort of auto-prophesied warning and fled. She was gone for five days. Was that the week the neighbours on one side started peering into the garden and tutting? And the neighbours on the other side started sending strange notes about 'unforgivable noise?' I couldn't put things in order. I had to triangulate them. Complaints from neighbours are also transactions, but you can't eat them. I was hungry and didn't know what to do. Hot do.

You are embarrassed

After the first day of your course you are greeted at the front door of your lodgings with a hug and an insult directed at your hair as the child takes things out of your shopping bag. Things repeat. Before the end of the welcome your can of soup is on the floor. You feel a little mugged but at the same time, flattered. Tonight, like every night, the girl is in the middle of a surge and her mother looks exhausted. An energy like that could crumble a ship. Let me in it, you think, you'd like to help. Help? To help and to have are getting confused. Even when leaping from armchair to sofa the girl has a kind of territorial generosity. Space follows her in madness. Maybe that's what's exhausting about children: her life force relies on the adult world for drainage. It's tiring to be anything other than the child, so you play, or attempt to. I would often move toy objects and blubber my lips too. She was younger then, a year is a long time for children, I couldn't interact so much but I used to pick up her dolls and get lost in their hypnotically dumb eyes until the girl bashed me on the head with a cushion. She bashes you on the head with a cushion. Things repeat. You say, That's not nice. She does it again but in slow motion with a song about lady elephants. Then she asks you about sex. You tell her to ask her mother. She realises you are uncomfortable and enjoys it. She picks up her dolls and makes them kiss, then makes them hump aggressively, bashing them and rubbing them, saying oooh oooh oooh. You begin to sit up and leave. As you do she asks, Is this your house? You say No it's not, it's yours and your mummy's house. She continues rubbing her dolls and asks it again with a deep seriousness.

* * *

As a body in a family centre, anything you just happen to do one day can quickly become part of the behaviour of the household. The time you get up in the morning has to fit in with a schedule already there but then other schedules respond to this. This is about more than showers and toilet flushing, but not much more than that. Plumbing integrated with personal and professional lives is the pattern matching of mixed domesticities. This is what the three of you now are, a mix of people plus dolls. How we cater for and clean ourselves will be convenient for another person we live with, or not. My childhood insomnia was bad for me but convenient for Moffa because I would tidy the house late at night. Your dedication to organic dairy is good for you but inconvenient for your landlady, so you'll have to stop that. It was handy for that same landlady that I drank black tea but bad for the cups and my teeth. I think I'm pushing the idea of convenience here, there isn't much about anyone's behaviour that's useful to someone else unless it's their work. What else are we except things for whoever we live with to put up with? For instance, I bang doors when I'm tired; you sneeze a lot; I spend a long time in the shower thinking, massaging my shoulders, tugging my nipples; you talk to yourself; I sigh when I piss; you hum when you brush your teeth; I miss payments by a day or two; you keep buying the girl chocolates; I used to swear in front of her; you heave-laugh; I drop things. We are what we do in the hours in between.

Here's what you routinely do by the end of your first week in the house: At the worst time of the morning a note scratches under your door that asks if you are awake. You are, you write back with a hurriedly found pen from your bag, 'I am.' When you open the door the girl is sitting on the floor scowling, surrounded by strips of school uniform and tights. This is a chance, an opportunity to be helpful and to belong to the house, and you want to be helpful. You step over her, miming f-i-v-e m-i-n-u-t-e-s with your hand. When you return from the shower the girl is on your bed playing with your phone, which is streaming the news in between songs. Boring boring voices, she says, *I hate the boring voices*. You dress in prudence while she glances at you and smirks, you move behind the wardrobe door and out of view. You knock your funny bone on the edge and with a wince do a small calculation about the rent for the room and the cost of privacy. When you are smart enough in your wraparound blouse she takes your hand and leads you downstairs, where it is still dark except for some small lights over a mirror. It is so warm. Every room is like baked milk that you sludge through, gratefully curdling in suburbia, the central heating so very, very on.

In the kitchen the girl chooses which cereal to have for the longest time possible, and she can. It's a test. You reach to the shelf above the fridge and wave your hand over the boxes: animal-themed frosty nuggets, toffee-flavoured cobbles, gimmick knobbles, wheat alien heads. They bring focus. Hmmm. You're moving your hand across the cereal boxes like I used to move my hand across the cereal boxes. I would not choose that one, too much like satanic totems in pink and green. It's like memory. Crunchy, sugary life you pour into her bowl until the girl makes her doll grunt and toy pig squeal over the side. Is that enough? you ask. *Not pretty!* She says this to you a lot. I wouldn't be offended. Her mother is groomed and beautiful even first thing in the morning. She says your eyes are dirty. Why are your eyes dirty? You explain that it's eye-liner while her doll's perfectly lashed eyes look up at you. I don't like it, she says. You puff out your cheeks and kiss the top of her head to shush her, like a parent would, you like to think. How many minutes have you got left until you have to leave? Are you stressed? Fill a glass up with water from the tap and see. You pick up a plastic ghost mask from the floor and hold it over your face as you sit down next to her to pour your muesli. She ignores you. You put the mask down.

Not pretty!

It is basically true, you're like the last doll lying around. After your breakfast you slide a bundle of £20 notes into a drawer and wonder whether you can leave the girl alone in the kitchen or not. You have to leave for your first class. There's a book about lions lying open on the table. She snatches it away and reads her invented passages, The lions are the dead lions, they are all lions. You go to say goodbye but are silenced with a pointed finger.

You shout a goodbye up the stairs at just the wrong volume, then hoist your bag onto your back before walking out. You have to be careful about what you say to children about promising to be back later on. But you will come back here, to where she scribbles and sings, you are committed to her by accident and it has woken something up. You have arrived somewhere, but not quite. You will be back later, moving into the slipstream. Soon you won't want to leave at all.

Moffa the return

It was a morning of chubby spiders and dewy webs. I walked up the long street of ex-council interwar terraces towards Moffa's house, finding every facade facile and jeering. I hadn't slept at all, the veering hedges felt dream-like. Pompous, I thought, too wet and puffed up. Was I walking slowly or quickly? I was walking like a nervous tourist, looking too much at other people, not wanting to be looked at myself. Some people had gloves on and others were dressed like it was summer. They were going to jobs. It wasn't yet 8 a.m. Approaching and entering Moffa's house needed to be crucially timed and this was far too early in the morning, so what was I doing? I started slowing down and rethinking my impulse to go straight there. Perhaps I should go to the supermarket first? The front gate I was lingering by opened. It was opened by Lloyd.

Lloyd used to live across the road but now lived down

the road from Moffa and all my life he'd turned up when I desperately didn't want to talk to anyone, especially him. When I was young he would come over to do things in the garden while I was daring to sunbathe, tasks that were hard work but essential and therefore ignored by Moffa. He was going to work. Shouldn't he be retired? His sad adoration of Moffa had spanned years despite her neglect of him. You're back then, he said, Nice to see you. Hello, I'm not sure. With so little sleep I found conversation difficult. You remember me? he said. I'm not sure. We all remember *you*. That's nice. You're back to see her? I'm back to see her. She's all right? No … I paused, Is she? Then said, I don't know, yes, she might be, she might be all right. I nodded at my sensible statement. Lloyd tapped his Tupperware and said, She'll be glad to see you anyway. I am on my way there now, I said, and stumbled a little. Mind out, it's that way. Yes. Careful. Thanks. Are you OK? I'm on my way to the shop now. He looked sad, he held his belt and lunchbox and said, You wouldn't think that woman could ever be far from all right from the way she belts out some Cher at Madden's karaoke nights. He was trying to make me smile.

I couldn't let men like Lloyd back in the story. Cautiously I'd reveal myself in trips to the shops. I'd tell Moffa I was back tomorrow. I'd go to her house tomorrow. I'd take her some bread. Today I would get food.

Instead of the shop I went back to my flat and got into bed. I lay there until midday having imaginary conversations with people. My circumstances have changed, as I explained to people I imagined asking me questions on the high street.

My circumstances have changed, I wrote it in emails in response to past lovers and bosses. My circumstances have changed, the flush doesn't exactly work brilliantly here but ... it's cheap! My circumstances have changed, it's not a very large town, there's a train once an hour, the shops are fine, a new café has opened. Great to be back! I assessed my life. I was back. This is what I do. I visit cities and think I live there. I walk around them fascinated with a bag over my shoulder, believing I am unstuck from the permanent returning to what has felt since childhood like an eternal armpit. I take myself out to a famous square, wander around a museum on a lunch break needing to go to the toilet or to take a photo, I get a job, I try something, then come to my senses as it all fails and head off, fold the beginning of a life up and shoo myself into transit. Not unstuck, stuck still. The long streets of cities, the institutions, the people were exciting but I needed to get back in order to become again the one who returns, because that's who I am. Every time I return I have to explain to myself that where she lives was always my destination. Each life I had before was just a short story to put inside me, every new start a failure, and each temporary address was one head on top of a beast of multiple heads. Is this making sense?

I collected theories of how to be employed or person-like, how to believe in locks and keys, to be part of the nucleus inside that stalks the circumference, with love, the combination of sauntering while remembering to quit leaving, and then returned from there to this small town where Moffa lived. That's what I mean. When I say, Bye bye life,

I was your caravan, I came here but I've got to go now, I am simply being myself. Moffa was the gravity that was picking me up, then knocking me back over, from which I am never leaving, never going far from or for very long. Yes, it's a bind but if you'd been there then, in those days, if you'd been in that triangle, you'd keep returning. If you'd heard what the neighbours called her, you'd count the steps away from and then back to her. And if you had felt worry even before your brain could understand what that feeling was, and instead coded worry right into your sense of place, then you wouldn't leave either, because the feeling never leaves you. I'm only now all these years later wondering how being worried and being away allows me to play on a small act of leaving, to soon start being a metaphorical house that's built on top of my memory of her, that I go off and try to recreate but can't, and how that is itself a feeling that's homely. Yes, worry is homely so I don't really leave. I just finish my affairs in whatever city or life, imaginary and theoretical, and head back. I polish off a plate of pastries, sticky and sweet, abandon friends, and get off. I break the rules and take myself away in order to return again. You'd stay close too, and you wouldn't be able to imagine being gone or elsewhere either if the feeling of leaving never left you. The feeling is standing in the house on top of her. Coming back to it gradually in different ages. Let me start that again. You might wonder why I'm so compelled as well as terrified to be here. You've heard of mothers haven't you?

You're comfy

Let me tell you, on this side of time, beyond the lodging, it's all mothers and no children. Children are myths. They are illustrations on plates. They smile out of windows. They laugh on the other side of the park. They are animated and glowing in films that I switch off right at the moment a mother scoops them up into loving arms. You're still there, in the nook of the undivided.

It is your fifth morning in the house and your dress is over your head. As your arms are raised, the girl runs into your bedroom with an urgent question, Are you our manager? You say, No, absolutely not. She argues that you are. I am not your *manager*, you tell her with your dress over your head, That's silly. She is upset by this. Screeching, shouting, jumping up and down saying, Yes you are, yes, yes, yes you are! She darts away without closing your door, and you hear her run through the house to the kitchen where her mother is. A minute later she comes back in again with a clever smile. *Lodger,* she says. You hug her and lift her up, That's it. The humblest word. Lodger, a particularly mortal word. Lodger, a slightly naughty word. Lodger. A critterish word. Something furry crawls out of it.

Downstairs the mother is moving boxes and sighing. As soon as she feels you are in the room her face reels in, she smiles at you like you're a customer in her shop. Are you all right? Did you sleep well? So well, you say, So well. She smells like cocoa butter. You don't offer to help with the boxes or even wonder what they are.

* * *

You're getting comfortable in the daily routine of going to your course and coming back. Weekdays are safe and fantastically the same at every hour. Early morning, before school, after school, teatime, before bed, bedtime. If you are not the one who has to administer these discrete identical episodes, you can enjoy the security they produce. Feed from it even, like playing with dolls.

The fact of the little girl is a thrill, her existence, just the way she coughs and moves her eyes, shocks you. Shock not from how loud she is or how quickly she transforms from sitting still to screaming and running—that's when you're in the room—it's the simple fact of her song-voice, of her speaking, of her conducting her thoughts and having eyelashes. Her bends and speeds, the smooth purpose in her feet. You, on the other hand, are lumbering, fool-bonded to rules. What's fascinating to you is the role you play in this house with a mother and child. To have a role at all! It feels strange. You are part of the house that orbits the child and her matters. She has systems and alarms and dimensions that you've stepped into, and regardless of you, nothing that's supposed to be structural seems able to manage her.

In the early hours of the night you hear her run across the landing, which winces. She thunders in and out of the toilet, the light-switch string whacks the wall. You sense that the house can hardly hold her, like a piano with a cat running up and down its keys. She is not in the hour, the hour is looking for her, it is one step behind. The din she makes is becoming homely to you. Every room except yours constantly asks after her, what set of clothes she has on and whether she is inside it or out there, if she is about to hurt herself, whether she is eating food and if it needs wiping off.

Right now she sits quietly making a cardboard book of her favourite names. At nothing she gasps, runs upstairs, runs back down with a radio. You can't see the logic. You feel as unmoving as a chair. She is a bundle of decisions you have and haven't made looking up at you, jumping out at you from behind a wall, playing the radio loudly in your face. Otherwise she is nothing. Once you've slopped upstairs and your door is closed she is barely more than a noise on the outside of your life. Things add up in you in the wake of her. She is fundamental but children are so nearly not there. They are solid and flickering, coming about because of hardly anything. Like someone who nearly dropped a plate, or how I narrowly avoided getting a fine on a train last month, I almost had children one day, someone else almost didn't, you might and you might not.

In the meantime lodgers lie under the surface of these events like sunken boats, wobbling between mud and water. We study ourselves through the movements of others then turn over. I used to sit in the same bedroom as you are in now, on the bed, leaning against the back wall, listening to the girl on the other side swoosh up and down the bathtub.

In what way does it make you aware of yourself as not there? Organless and yet slopping, full of blank solutions like a barrelfish, madly at counsel but saying nothing. You hear a small foot drag along the side of the bath making the plastic squeak, then the muffled voice of the mother going into the bathroom with a warm towel, the tune of their shared jokes, the duetted *hu-bŭ-bu-bu-buh* as the girl's arms and legs are rubbed dry. My heart does beat. The wall. Thank goodness, I think. And you too, with your small can of beer and book. We feel a small hate, but for which one, mother or child? Resentment for what they can't share with my young self, the one that's stuck, still skulking in the hull.

You. You've fallen asleep. Does nothing touch you? You were uncomplicatedly nurtured as a child and it has made you a little dumb. If you went back to your family address right now, if you showed up at your childhood door, someone would let you in and say, Hiya, then carry on with what they were doing. A little later on someone else might ask how you are and what you're up to these days, you'd briefly try to explain as their eyes drift back to the TV. So now you are sleeping sitting up, eyes closed, mouth open, snoring against the noises of another family's bath time. It is, what can we call it? Unalienating. The noises of others give you sound to retreat from without disturbing your sense of place in the world. Am I close? Am I spot on?

Moffa the house

TODAY I WILL GO TO MOFFA'S HOUSE, I said to myself. I woke up having hardly slept again and felt trapped. There was no food in the cupboards. This was the fifth day of living here and I hadn't really bought anything except soap, tea bags and a large ready-made couscous salad that I ate a mouthful of whenever I passed the fridge. The couscous salad was drying. I set off and traversed the small market town in the strangest way, avoiding Moffa's house completely at first, walking essentially in loops: past a Co-op for a cheese pasty, through the leisure centre car park and down an alley I didn't know was there. It led to a side street that I vaguely recognised, then to a fence I climbed under and to another car park at the back of her street. I finally let myself arrive at her door in the afternoon feeling nervous and still hungry. Her house had things about it I'd forgotten I loved, like the sound of the gate opening; and repellent elements I could never forget, like the rest of it. This feeling I had when I went there was the sort of thing we read about on our course: this was what locks us up indoors, in rooms—the maternal soul at the centre of every house. And what locks us out is something else. Is it the paternal design at the starting point of every habitation? Is that too much? The two elements can be the same parent, or no one in particular. It might be where the towels are kept or it might in the plaster, nesting in the roof, but one outdoes the other. One parent pulls us into the lounge and makes us drink, while the other creates restlessness, worry about memories we don't want to have, and makes us want to leave again. You might think this is a basic formulation, but anyway, the house is all mother, carpets and bed linen, while the domain, the father, is the reason we can't look in mirrors at night. That's why I was always spinning around on the hoof of having-just-left and on the hoof of having-just-got-back. Returning, returning. I couldn't bear her but I couldn't stop worrying about her. That's why I was back, standing at the door of the house that revolted me and drew me in. You should tell me what it all means, you're the one who's studying now, learning how to go into our pasts, how to turn its burnt-on images into therapeutic techniques. Hope you get further with it than I did. (I imagined giving someone a head massage, I said, *What a horrible night you had, there, that's better isn't it?* I giggled in their ear.)

I rang the bell to Moffa's front door and could sense I'd disturbed absolutely nothing. I pressed it again, imagined saying, Hello, surprise! I'm sorry I didn't call. I'm sorry I'm here. I'm fine are you OK? I'm fine, are you OK? I'm fine. I don't want anything. Are you OK? Shut up, stop asking that. There was no one in. I was suddenly very hungry. I went around the back of the terrace along a long, narrow passage and through the gate of her small garden. I let myself in through the back door using the only key I'd managed to hold on to in my life. Stepping into the kitchen to where a radio was mumbling a terrible-sounding play, I circled the lino a few times then got on with sussing out the health and sustainability of her living situation. First, I opened a madeira cake and ate a slice. There was a bowl of marbles on the side next to some recipe books. I poured the marbles into another bowl, discovered nothing, poured them back into the first bowl, switched the kettle on. On the fridge there was a photo of Moffa in a line of women of all different ages wearing matching T-shirts and smiling. Who were they? I counted twelve lamps, each one dangerous-looking in its own way, an even cheaper version of the cheap papery standing lamps that everyone has, each one dusty, each a potential fire hazard, a lamp with a fat glass base on the edge of a tiny table, a very old side-leaning standing lamp with a skew-whiff shade. Granted the room did have a nice opaline glow when I switched them all on. It was then I realised how carefully placed they were, stage-crafted to catch the materialising lines of her clutter; the population of ornaments, ranges of candleholders and souvenirs, even an empty chocolate box now full of wrappers was lit to its best. A Venetian mask had a dead incense stick coming out of its eye socket.

A pile of bent-open romance novels and loose CDs had caught the ash. This was just the kind of carefully decorated destruction Moffa made homely. It confused me so I sat down. As soon as I sat down—and I can't be indoors for long without folding up into a chair and yawning—it got too much like I had arrived, so I had to leap into the stance of someone who leaves. An embarrassment was creeping through me that needed suppressing. I made myself a tea.

The dirty spoon and other disgraces suggested that either Moffa's ability to care for herself was declining, or that all was the same as it has always been. I found: a second radio on its side in the pot of a houseplant, a dangerously old block of cheese in the fridge, unopened letters, dozens of them, and in the garden I found a sputniky barbecue that was so rusty it made my teeth sing to be near it. The garden had a lot going on. A late-blooming passion plant was pouring out high and low. I followed its climbing fingers along the three fences to the warped back door that would only shut with a shove. Back inside, I paced the two cramped rooms, satisfied, just, then went upstairs, ignored the two bedrooms but stepped into the tight skylit bathroom that had a bathtub but no shower. It did have many flavoured oils and gels; everywhere the musk and Moffa's obtruding body. I stepped through one paradigm after another; an overflowing bathroom bin, the smell of lavender, peeling bits of the wall, an airing cupboard full of very pretty frayed towels; the living imbalance of health and decoration. Everywhere's mess was a mark of either her attention or her neglect, so earthed by her hand and buzzing loudly with her weird life. There was no sign of shame in any of the objects or their placement, nothing effacing about the habits and practices within the daily spending of a state pension. No nervous tidying or pasting over of the self, but enhancers and embellishments of it. I opened the bathroom cabinet. That was a trespass. There was nothing in there except the spoils of unextraordinary visits to the chemist for what an older woman's skin and hair naturally and riotously does, as well as some make-up, which is the same thing. A tube of unopened vitamins rolled out into the sink. I took some sheets from her airing cupboard.

Downstairs and back in the armchair I got too comfortable again, I was hot and unfolding. I unclenched and felt myself in the repressions made by Moffa's body and all her hours of relaxation watching detective dramas. I nearly fell asleep. I would have fallen deeply to sleep but the doorbell rang. Not a ding-dong but a hard, alarming bringing. The sound went straight to my gut. It always sounded like someone angry and violent had arrived. What? I shouted in my half-sleep. I got up and opened the door with squinting eyes. O, hello. A man who was both a musician and a mechanic and who wore the combined costumes of both stood before me. It was Madden, in a baseball cap, with longer, much whiter hair flowing greasily from it. I can't explain Madden, his voice was nearly as loud as Moffa's, he smelt of rolled cigarettes and he was carrying a bag. Two questions! he said. I nodded. Do you like sausage rolls? I felt ill, really peculiar, something like déjà vu shook my legs. It's my new project to make 'em from scratch, he said and held the bag open. I nodded again, the smell of pork and fat making me queasy. Second question, Madden clicked his fingers and said, Do you like pub quizzes? I looked past him at the sky, I tried to find a horizon. I was very sleepy and confused. Lloyd saw you come in, he said, so I thought I'd bring these round for you. No, it's OK, thank you. There was a pause, Madden held the bag of sausage rolls open. Sure? Yes, mhm. And what about the quiz? Umm, I don't think it's for me. O yes it is, it's on Monday, in the Beehive. Be there at seven!

I closed the door slowly and sat down against the wall. The thought of Lloyd seeing me walk here was too much. The thought of Lloyd informing Madden made me very angry. After about half an hour of triangulating I got up, poured the marbles back into my preferred bowl and left Moffa's house with the sheets.

You are revolted

One evening you say, Can I have my glasses back, please? The girl will laugh because that's not her language. You could become strict, speak with an adult's power of language, but you're hesitant to and she senses this, so she laughs again and you hate her. You feel drained and bored. They cost £103 and I need them, you say, they are the most expensive things I own, you try, they could break and then I won't be able to see writing. Please give them back. *No!* For some reason tonight the girl stinks. A sickly mix of sulphur and piss. The wax in her ears and the grease in her hair have blended together with some urethral steam, making her pungent and repulsive. Perhaps a child's attitude and odour are connected, you wonder. Whatever it is, at this moment you feel no affection for her at all. You are revolted by her clammy little hands. She writes out a word with her pens, you patiently watch her until she holds it up: *beeepoill.*

What does that say? You sigh, Nothing. *Wrong!* Please. *No*. Please. No, I'm a manager, she says and pretends to poo on the floor. You notice she has a cut on her knee and some white cream has been rubbed on it. The sight of the slick emollient on the slimy wound makes you feel worse, you imagine a long, gungy finger with a painted fingernail tapping cream onto the cut skin. The whole house feels revolting.

You go to snatch the glasses off her face, feeling like her squabbling sister, she swishes her head away and they fall onto the floor. Great, thank you very much, you hiss and hate the sound of your voice. Her smile has shrunk but it's still there, wryly, and she's looking at you as you pick up your glasses like you've misunderstood something. It's a little bit like pity, the look, and it doesn't feel misplaced. Without saying anything the girl returns to her pens and continues inventing words, curling and bending her letters grotesquely. She starts translating the words into a song which you realise, as you step away and up the stairs, is about you. Fuck you, you little shit, is what you mutter on the stairs, wiping your glasses on your sleeve.

When you reach your bedroom you find your landlady's treatment table is still up. It's usually been dismantled and folded away by now, like it was never there at all. The sight of the table reveals the other life of the room. It looms explicitly, testament to privateering and need. You want to collapse it, but very quietly. If the legs clatter the mother will hear and realise she left it out. Even tonight you want to protect her from that delicate shame, from having to rush in and fold the table herself. Before you try to find a catch or lever you pause at the table. You hold its edges which remind you of a waist, then push down on its creamy smooth couching. It feels so strong and tender that you fold yourself over it and breathe with your mouth open onto the vinyl surface, quietly, crawl all the way onto the treatment table and lie on your front, letting your whole body weigh down into the soft thick padding. This is where we meet. In these moments we are the same. Your body has to find cradles in accidents like mine does. It's your own mass that pushes you down, that pushes back. You try to weigh more. This is true rest. You turn your head to the side and gaze at the door then fall asleep. I see you so clearly because I've laid myself out on that table too.

Moffa the café

The unfortunate characteristic of all regional towns is that they are very definitely *in* Britain. You can forget this country exists in cities. Concepts like England are less relevant; all cities belong to each other worldwide. Where are you when in a city? Nowhere and everywhere. Buzzing on a unique time zone. But towns? They're in the country, they're part of it, they *are* it. Little nation devices. All towns are model towns. Half the population of a town likes it like that, they'd crawl even more into the tenets and tents of Great Britain if they could. Others are so stunned by the impoverishing effects of their own town on them that they don't think about it, can't think about it. Their counterparts are either shame-dumb or gut-dumb from the richness of the town's resources they hoard. Some are young and are *trying* something. Not in a city but in a town would you walk into a new café, run by a young, good-looking couple, and think, O good for them! And what's more, good for me for coming in here and making it even better for them. Good for me for them. Service and supply. Disproportionate egos and one's role in the overall mood. A town. Hello, one tea please.

Like a baby I still drank tea. Because tea was still cheap and coffee made me excited and then panic about dying. The café I had come into wasn't really set up to sell just 'a cup of tea,' when I ordered the college-age kids had to move differently in their rehearsed chain of false barista gestures. They gave me large sweet smiles as I paid. The café I had come into was on the high street on my way back from Moffa's empty house and I needed to catch up with myself. The word 'inspire' was written in a slightly darker cream on the cream-coloured feature wall. I sat down near the window and thought, This place used to be a hairdresser's. It was called Salon Confidence. I wondered if Moffa ever came in here to celebrate her town's new café and get lipstick all over her latte's glass cup. She probably did come in here and talk loudly about her past. Other people's conversations would be drowned out, they'd be annoyed at first then find themselves listening in to her story about a long-ago love affair. Delicious stranger gossip. I had none. The tea and the café's big sunny window made me sweat. A little sweaty, I realised I was staring at people. First at a group of laugh-filled friends, men and women in their late seventies, each with a slice of cake—one slice was bright green and they all looked amused by it. On the other side of me, I stared at two young mums. I stared at their croissants, I was hungry. My gawping soon caught their eye and I instantly understood how messy my hair was. We all looked away and I felt alone. From the window I saw that the townsfolk who were not in the café were on the streets, marching around with heavy reused shopping bags, coming in and out of Wilko, Iceland and Superdrug. The couples looked deeply pissed off with each other, long-term, hunched and exhausted. I watched them vibrate at the crossing, yell at each other, stand by a bench and sort their shoe out, lift a child up, scratch their arms. The view had become completely entrancing when a large man's back eclipsed it. Curves from a thick, tanned neck into an Aertex T-shirt, wide leather belt in jeans. It was Madden. He was finishing a cigarette and blocking my view—as if on purpose. The angle of his white-tendrilled head suggested a worldly vantage on things. I watched him flick his rollie onto the ground and then walk through the café doors and right up to my table.

I'm just busy. Hello again, he ignored me. Yes hi. What do you think of this place, eh? Pretty hipster? Very handy and not too expensive, I replied and wished I had something to look down at to read. So, he slapped his hands on his thighs, can I count on you for Monday night? There'll be a theme. You'll like it. I'm quite tired actually. No, young thing like you should be out and enjoying life. Not young, tired. Lots of people will be pleased to see ya. I don't think I can. He sang a little song, O o o say you will, say you won't … He pointed at me and held the point as he paced away from me backwards, You're going to love it, it'll be a great night.

Madden had walked backwards nearly all the way to the door when he bumped into someone, a woman in a mauve jacket, dyed red hair and a pot plant. Hello Meany love, he cooed, you look well. Meany didn't say much but looked up at Madden's earring and smiled and said, Mmm. Madden kissed her cheek. Meany went, Hehe, I have a shamrock. He held his arm around her and pointed at me, Look who it is, guess who? O? ... Meany said as her thick mascaraed eyes widened and narrowed at me.

September in a town in this country. Bad luck. A wrong ache of a country. An angry old nation sitting in an armchair swatting at nothing. I too was part of its corduroy, so was this town and this café. Let's line up and collect the biscuit crumbs. After a drizzly walk I entered my building and stomped up the stairs, considering all the tragedies of a pub quiz.

You make crumpets

You've been lodging with the mother and child for nearly two weeks, often left in charge for an hour or two while your landlady shops or works in the late afternoon and evening. The arrangement is working, you feel special, getting more from these moments than from your course. Gradually more at ease with this child, you grill cheese onto a crumpet, slice an apple, go over the spelling of 'ph' words. You dial your hips around the kitchen and admit that you are impersonating a mother. A really good one, a mother who enjoys long conversations with her self-knowing offspring.

It's a surprise to find that sometimes talking to the girl is immediately boring. Silly, but in a tedious way. What if you push through that? Will there be a bond? Is that what you think? Consider it work. Not all that satisfying but perhaps creative work, a conversation similar to sculpting: all hands are leading the form so the topic can turn magnificent, go crude or become rigidly stubborn. You have to protect the topic but also be willing for your hands to break it, to let them guide the shape or stick things into the shape and ultimately allow for it to become what they want—a miniature depiction of you as a fool: I'm doing farts in my mind. How was your day? Where is Mummy? She'll be back soon. The girl turns to you, You have to guess what I'm thinking. I can't guess, please don't make me guess. Try! Is it purple? you ask, like you're in pain. Umm no. Is it a number? Ummm. (What does a girl think about?) Will you remember me? you ask, like you're in pain. Yes a number. I'll think about you forever. Keep guessing! (What does a woman know?) I don't know. It's lots of small things. I'm not sure I know you at all. (No one fantasy can find another.) A number of ... ? Just tell me. Fish! Fish? They are in trouble. Because? They forgot ... They forgot what? Their brother. But? But? (I don't know.) Why did they forget him? They don't like him. Why? He's dead. And? The mummy fish will eat them. (Imaginations are as incompatible as love.) All the fish? Their willies first. OK, that's enough. Let's make up a number. I'm too tired to make up a number. Yes, guess it. Is it purple? (All dreams are a kind of loss.) A big purple number. What? A triangle. Do you want some of this carrot? What are fish? Sea life, endangered. Fish are boys, we eat them. Sometimes, yes ... The mummy will poo out their willies. No. They grow into schools and churches. How was your day at school? That's where me and you get married. And that's what you were thinking?

Moffa the rain

Today in my hometown it rained. I left the house four times, the first time I saw Lee Martin, a boyfriend from when I was eighteen and on a month-long return to Moffa. He had two sulky dogs with him. He talked to me like I had never been away, dropping names I didn't remember together with ones I did that made me cringe. He told me I should come to Dooley's fortieth birthday party and I burst out laughing. Lee Martin looked at me blankly. At the Working Men's Club. The second time I went out I bought a newspaper and a nail file, the third time I bought shampoo and toilet rolls, the fourth time I looked at the ducks. Each time I went out I looked more like a woman, more attractive to myself and in control. I will tell her I am back tomorrow. I will take her some duck eggs and offer to wash her hair. Where did that come from? Probably a film. I walked through the park in the fine drizzle. There was a noticeboard, and right in the middle was a horribly made poster advertising Madden's pub quiz. In tubular lettering it said: General Fun and General Knowledge! Huge Prizes!

You play with Milly

At a woolly hour of late morning you and the girl are sitting at the top of the stairs listening to the doorbell ringing over and over. She is threatening to throw her doll down the stairs. The child says to her doll, Milly, stop, you are stupid. You stand up and go into her bedroom and say, Come on, let's play in here. She turns to look at you with a worried weight in her eyes, and doesn't move. You take the doll out of her hands, Heeeey, she says. You dance the doll into her bedroom like a puppet, Where's Milly going? Oo what's Milly doing? She's flying into your bedroom. O no she's eating your bedcovers, o no! Milly's not well ... The doorbell stops ringing. You lean out of the girl's bedroom. It starts again, more aggressively in short punches. You sigh and bring Milly back to the girl, sit down next to her wondering what to do. The girl whispers into your ear with both hands narrowing her squeaking breath right into your canals, We are not allowed to open the door. I know, you snap, then assure her that you're not going to open the door, and add, Because I really don't care who's there. I don't care, she says, Milly doesn't care. She looks like she might cry. *Jesus Christ.* Wait for me in your bedroom, take Milly, don't come out. Then without friendliness, with no love at all, you say, Just do it for goodness' sake. You want to get an idea of who's there, that's all. Other than that you are happy to stick to the mother's instruction not to let anyone in while she's away. She'd said it three times as she inspected the car keys in her hand, forgetting they were there, looking at them again. She'd said, And don't answer the phone ... I know you wouldn't but don't let her pick it up ... Keep her upstairs. Your landlady had seemed far away, like she was on a dim moon battling instincts. She's happy she has someone dependable around, and you're so dependable because you're simply around. So why did she give you a look of someone who had recognised an enemy? All of the mother's looks are short-lived. She'd smiled and got in her car.

Now someone is at the door. When it first rang you were playing with tessellating bricks on her bedroom floor. You were happy to ignore it and do as you said you'd do. But then it continued abnormally, with no let-up, like the person who was ringing had done this before. You've already been alone with the child for nearly two hours and she's drained your energy like a lemon. If it was me I would want to get a sense of who was ringing too, I'd be brave I think. Do you have more respect for the rules than me? I keep finding these differences and it makes me sad. In fact you walk straight down the stairs, into the living room, and look directly at the door. Well now. You sense someone with a bullish determination, with an acceptance of time passing or even possession of it. He—it is a man—could do this all day. Then he slaps the letterbox a couple of times, then rings the doorbell repeatedly at the same time. I'm not sure, do you walk to the door? What *are* you doing? There's a light shining on your face. Do you answer the door?

Ten minutes later you go back up the stairs to find the girl in her bedroom standing on the doll's head.

Poor Milly.

She's a piss.

Poor Milly.

Moffa in my head

I know how to hide, it's very funny.

Who are you hiding from? Don't ask, just duck.

Judy Duck?

Yes, hide from Judy Duck. She wants our television and car. She came over and you're a big tart, Moffa.

Go to bed.

I'm worried you won't come back. What else?

I ate the bread dough.

You iron

Will you kiss my daddy? she asks. I'm sorry? The girl is sitting in the dark, alone at the breakfast bar. She has been waiting for you. You draw the curtains and switch the kitchen light on. Have you met my daddy? You tell her it's Thursday, Do you like Thursdays at school? She doesn't answer, she asks, What does your daddy look like? You say, Like a polar bear with a big tummy and a dimple on his chin. WHAT? A dimple. She twiddles her loose hair then says, My daddy is a handsome devil, and a ffff-uckah. You laugh then quickly stop. She continues, I've *met* him. You have? Twice: one time when I was a baby and once with ice cream but I can't remember. I'm going to kiss him, are you? You say, O I doubt it, but in your mind you are kissing her daddy. You are kissing him in the kitchen right now. A man in an old blue dressing gown, whose chin scratches yours and who strokes your arms. The girl is still talking but you are lost in the fantasy. To begin with you are his lover, then his wife and together you have a little girl, like this real one glaring at you, who wants her breakfast. She is your daughter. She is colouring in a star and doesn't speak again for a few minutes while you pour stuff into a cup and bowl. You want to quickly iron your trousers and not think about kissing but it's too late. It is time to answer, Yes OK then I will, I'll kiss your daddy too. It feels safe to let him exist while her mother is still sleeping. There is no reply. The imaginary daddy has his arm around you. She says, No, you cannot marry my daddy, you are not pretty. OK, I won't. Where is your car? She asks this every day. I don't have one. She gasps like a pantomime horse then lowers her head in slow motion onto the colouring book. The imaginary daddy kisses your head and pours some more cereal into the girl's bowl. He clears his throat then drinks a glass of water at the tap, happy to be ignored. The ironing board makes a hee-haw sound and you miss her next question. Something about learning to swim. The imaginary daddy comes over, kisses your hand and then the iron, he licks your trousers, rubs his hand up and down the leg, breathes on the crotch. You iron him away.

At the breakfast bar the girl is trying to brush her hair in the handheld mirror but it's really a performance, she is finding her way to herself. The mother is nearly in the room. When she arrives the girl's hair will be transferred back to its creator and swiftly pulled into a ponytail, or pigtails, or a trio of little buns, the wisps around her forehead will be clipped with a little butterfly clip, or scraped back with an

Alice band. She'll do it with brusque habit. When does a mother plan her daughter's hair? Is it improvised? Is it decided the morning before? There are some things you will never know. As her head tugs back and forth the girl burps and claps both hands to her mouth. Her mother says her name in joke outrage, instructs the girl to be polite in front of you then laughs. You make some coffee to share and help plait the little girl's hair into double braids, while the girl holds the mirror to her face and does impersonations of the 'snobby' neighbours. The mother finds it hysterical, she holds the plaits steady and wipes her eyes on her shoulder, kisses her daughter's neck. And you laugh along too. The three of you are together and laughing; mother, daughter, lodger. You finish your coffee and prepare to leave. At the door the imaginary daddy kisses you deeply and puts his hand on your ass.

Moffa the farmer

A week after Madden brought sausage rolls I went to Moffa's house again. I hadn't managed to sleep much at all in my new bed and my instincts were goosey. I couldn't stick to one direction. To avoid Lloyd I walked a different way from before. Round the back of the leisure centre and through the park, along the side of a Catholic school and into then quickly out of a graveyard. It took over an hour to get there and when I arrived Moffa was not in, again. But this time I expected that to be the case. I was pleased. It was peaceful. I made myself a tea and sat in her armchair and turned her TV on. After a long TV programme about bears I turned over to ITV2 only to be confronted with a repeat of a crime drama with Moffa in it. She was playing the wife of a heavily indebted gambling-addict farmer who was about to murder a whole load of people. Moffa only had a few scenes before the farmer killed her with a spade. Their teenage daughter wept over her large costumed corpse at the police station as she identified her. I recognised the girl immediately and choked. Her pretty green eyes, her delicate arms and neat skin. I turned over to the news.

You put on tights

It is not yet seven in the morning as you thread a child's leg through some thick yellow tights and feel as normal as a fridge. It is a kind of benign beingness you are happy to pay for. She is lying on her back acting younger than she is and pretending she will kick you but feigning some gentleness at the last moment. Ignoring her kicks you ask some questions about places in the world she might like to go to one day. She taps her foot on your chest saying, Here, here, here. You tell her about a city in Asia where monkeys wander the streets and sit next to people on park benches, sometimes stealing their books. She is imagining it and has gone quiet then asks to see a picture of a monkey on your phone. There's a sweet silence while she imagines herself in a fantasy that you gave her and that is now becoming hers. A man's voice ruins the moment. Hello, it says, here we all are then. From on the floor the child casually waves to the man who has walked into the room then carries on playing with your phone with her other hand. The man stands over you smiling, unfortunately and loomingly, with office trousers and a stripy blue shirt. You've never seen him before, but he's typical.

This man is Professor Dommer, a doctor of memory, or something. He is standing there. The mother is still sleeping and cannot explain or introduce him so the child assumes a way to do it. He is a man with a car and ginger eyebrows who knows about brains and who stays here too. He prefers blue milk. He arrived with his milk preference while you were at your friend's house at the weekend, leaving a fat leather jacket on the hook. The memory professor stays on Tuesdays, Wednesdays and alternating Fridays. He pays more for a bigger bedroom—a bedroom you had until this second understood to be a storage room cut out of the garage with a door that wouldn't open due to fullness. It had been laboriously adapted into a bedroom without you noticing and now has a double bed and a small table with a kettle thronged by biscuits and sachets of instant coffee, all of which you might like to sometimes sneak in to pinch as I would like to sneak in to pinch. Towels are laid out on the bed more in the manner of the service of invisible employees. The bed linen and curtains are brand new, made of a cheap fabric still with packet-pressed folds, fit for the business of charged sleeping.

The three of you move in sequence from the living-room floor into the kitchen, where the professor plays out a routine of knowing where everything is. He gets a plate out of the cupboard and a mug down from the correct shelf, he pours out some instant coffee into the mug without using a spoon. He offers you very little attention and sets his briefcase carelessly down on top of your bag. You glare at the briefcase mounting your bag while he makes stupid jokes with the girl. His questions sound ignorant and clunky to you but are spoken in the manner of someone who knows how to talk to children, knows so well, is good with them, is so at ease with them. He makes stupid voices. In comparison you are quite stiff. You jump down from the stool and take your bowl of muesli to eat alone in the bedroom that is yours for fifteen more minutes. After that your room will be used to wax your landlady's clients, while the professor's bedroom will be kept shut to protect his things. He has no things. A razor maybe. Professor Dommer is the first man to set foot in the house in the short, eclectic time you've spent here. Wasn't this to be a house without men? But the girl doesn't seem too excited about him, it's you who's bothered. It's you who can't stand his stories about evolution sprayed over her picture books or the way he holds his toast.

Moffa the sounds

Back in my sublet I wasn't sure whether it was day or night. There were no legible rhythms to either, time was full of faces peering at me and flashes of recognition. I thought I heard Kav come in. I rolled off my bed, embarrassed to have been so entrenched there during the possible day. The last thing I wanted was to meet Kav when I was confused. Was that a thump and a slam? Was it Kav trotting through the kitchen while I was in bed, pouring rice into his bin-liner mouth? Did some spill on the floor? The slamming noise happened again. It was from the floor below. A friend of mine told me once, when I was upset about a noisy flatmate in my twenties, that we needed to hyper-empathise with the faceless people who disturb us. For instance we should say to ourselves, that bastard needs to play his music right now at that volume because he's had a terrible nightmare and he suffers from anxiety that's eased if he dances on the spot. Or, that disgusting slob behind me on this train is eating crisps so noisily because he's hungry, he didn't have time to eat today, he's rushing from work, his name is Nico and he's on his way to the bedside of his sick daughter who is on nil by mouth and he doesn't want to eat in front of her. Or, that arsehole screams at her cats because she loves them so much, and she's a war veteran. She's an alcoholic. Her heating has been cut off.

You fall asleep

And you, who are you beyond your living standards? If there is such a thing. What songs do you like and what choices did you have and not have to get you here? The colour of your knickers: blue, I reckon. I imagine you are a worrier. But not like I am, one single person hasn't absorbed all your worry into a lifelong madness. I imagine that you stare at the thing that worries you. For instance, you can't take your eyes off the vulnerable person on the bus, you check your bank balance multiple times a day. You call one of your siblings after every bad dream. They are so bored of you. Your parents live unflinchingly as a married couple, their still-living parents are interchangeable. Carpets and lampshades are cleaned professionally. Your dad comes in and shouts the name of his second-division football team as a greeting. Thinking about them brings you no fear.

Once more on this muggy evening, check your bank

statement, then close your laptop and try to relax. Finish eating your cheese with some cherry tomatoes then do your washing up. Dry the small plate you used and return it to the cupboard quietly. Brush away any crumbs. Look away from spaces where clothes are drying, look away from the unfriendly dog, move away from Professor Dommer, who has come to fry his evening eggs, look away from the blistering egg white. How will you relax? There are two women in your bedroom—one is having her bikini-line waxed by the other—still. You agreed to extend your stay out of the room for another two hours and to keep an eye on the girl, who has gawped everything out of existence except the TV. The professor is whistling. I agree, it would be nice after a long day spent under bright lights to lie down on the bed, to scratch your chest where your bra has been rubbing, to stroke your tummy where your waistband has been digging, enjoy a happy flatulence with headphones over your ears, a cup of instant hot chocolate in your hand as a reward for bothering. Instead you sit down on the sofa with the child, who snuggles into your side for your body heat, and attempt to follow the narrative of her favourite programme about a vengeful and unregulated animal law enforcement agency. The professor brings his plate of fried eggs with roasted squares of potato to the sofa to sit with you, to also watch the cartoon about a vengeful and unregulated animal law enforcement agency. You shift along some more, into the child. She sticks out her legs and lays them on you. You look over at the professor's eggs which would make you hungry were they not coated in a spicy orange sauce that puts you off. He eats unexpectedly quietly, he chuckles at the programme. Having prepared yourself to wish him into oblivion the closeness of his lap to your lap, overlaid with a child's kicks, is homely. With a certain effort you abandon sensitivities, you ease into the situation and also the cushions. Then—you see it—the reflection of the three of you in the television screen. It looks like a mock family. You are sitting in the correct shape but without the pressing chores or seething resentment. The light on the screen changes but the picture stays with you. The professor takes one of the girl's feet and holds it in his hand. He says, From tomorrow I'll be gone and won't see you for a week or two. Are you sick? No, he says, I'm going to Utrecht. You don't say anything, just look down at her foot in his hand and the plate of orange smears on his knees. It is finally possible to relax now that you cannot physically move from behind the barrier of a child's leg and a man's arm.

Moffa the liking

What I do is contrast one life with another. You, as I see you, resting your head on your arm and another head resting on you, have begun to hope for better. That's a single move. To hope for better. Just existing day to day will eventually make that hope, and the work you do in the name of it, fulfilled. My problem is I'm at one remove from this, or two or three removes. I hope to hope for better. In fact, I hope to hope to hope for better. That's called being stuck. How much of this is my own fault? Let's see. Very uncomplicatedly, I like three things: milkshake, reading epic novels, and my friend Judy. Simple things that I know I like and am happy to like, and yet none of them are in my life. I don't drink milkshake because I overthink its physical detriment, playing it off against the diminishing return of pleasure within the context of money; I am too lazy to begin reading lengthy books in case they turn out not to be worth it; Judy lives at the end of a long, expensive train journey that might turn out to be not worth it. Did I self-bind myself out of a good life or was it always too many moves away? I could go on. I believe I am playing the reward curve off against the luck dips, off against the willpower flips, off against the living constraints.

You hear words

The room is so hot you're not sure if you're asleep or awake. The air doesn't feel normal and what are these sensations? You feel part of something large and squashy, but bounded, bearing fragility. Radiators in a well-insulated house on a mild evening do things to the brain and skin. They draw moisture outwards and dry moods. You're empty and full, and vaguely remember a uniformed bear singing the same song over and over. And the professor. A hand on your leg? A leg on your leg? But the heat. There is pleasure. And another small body sleeping on you has made your senses spongy and your reactions droop. Your ego and underwear feel clammy then stiff, everything is sleepy then starchy. It is warm near the radiator with a sleeping child folded around you. The feeling makes sense of your bones, holding together a soft copy of you. There are voices from the front door that behave like auditory spirits. You hear the words: pores, party, credit card. The front door is open, the mother is saying goodbye to her customer who is also her friend. The girl's cub-like snoring mellows all sounds into a dream where you are component parts of one feathered animal within a cave, you are the same animal's torso that huffs and gently waits for planets to move. The dream is severed completely as one half of the animal is torn away. The mother lifts the girl up and away from your body, leaving you cold. The chill resembles each time in your life you have been rejected. You remain flop-armed and half-asleep on the sofa.

I'll see you in a week or so.

(He's talking to you.)

Hmm? *Yes.*

Leaning out of his bedroom the professor angles round to speak to you. He says something else then he says, *In a week or so.* You tell him good luck but you're fighting with unconsciousness. You look very sweet.

What?

In a week.

Yes, goodnight.

Moffa the leaving

The scowling small town had me by the ankles, pulling me down. I considered leaving but that felt too familiar, a dumb accident I was doomed to repeat. Madden had come to my flat. I don't know how he knew where I lived or how he'd got past the first doors but when I came back after an hour or so of sitting on Moffa's armchair there was a plastic box of very spicy-looking chicken curry on my doormat. It was full of bones and grease, great lumps of potato and chillies. On top was a homemade leaflet for the pub quiz. Seeing it made me furious. I went inside, searching idiotically for places to go and things to do on my phone: 'jobs in hospitals for women,' 'retreats for free in Scotland,' 'trains at night.' I calmed down and sat on the bed where I couldn't sleep or remember what my plan was, what my fate was. Who I was.

Who I was. Here's some context: I tried to leave Moffa when I was sixteen. I stopped being able to look at her. I started visiting the city near our town by bus, walking into grown-up pubs and ordering things for myself at the bar. I discovered that I liked to sit and crunch through a bag of salty crisps while doing a puzzle. That felt like me, so I elaborated on it. Eventually I found that I liked going into a particular pub where they let me pretend to be an adult, sitting at a table by the door, eating a bag of salt and vinegar crisps and drinking a lemonade into which I dropped a pickled onion, sometimes two pickled onions. So I could say to myself: what I like to do is this, and eat these, and I've brought myself here for just that. Sometimes a song came on the speakers that I enjoyed. My song, I like this. There wasn't room for these realisations in Moffa's house. Only in the city, and through my desire to eat crisps and drink lemonade with pickled onions in it, was I able to notice what I was allowed to want. There was a personality forming somewhere in the choice of one kind of crisp over another, and of an amount of onions in my lemonade; the timings, the flavour, the price. Would I rather have a bag now or later? Will it be nice? Why should I have crisps? Why shouldn't I? From these questions and observations it was a small leap into being a person. I felt like me. But me was someone who lived mainly on the verge of actions, someone who was always going to fall in between leaving and arriving, rationing and crunching. Could I be whole? Could I become the juicy singular triangle of my self: finance, pleasure and shelter?

I was someone who didn't have anywhere to put their stuff where they lived. I was a teenager who had a bedroom without any room for her things. My only base, the tiny room in Moffa's house, was a storage room, full of cabinets and boxes from Moffa's mother's flat after she died. Piles of large, stale coats and dresses, desiccating books and photo albums squatted about me like mumbling ancestors. The sliding doors of the fixed wardrobe were off their rails and would fall outwards, revealing packed-in bedding and more clothes. Some wigs. A younger girl could have played with it all, punched things and shoved herself into the wardrobe. But to me all the clutter felt like being screamed at.

Sometimes even that bedroom was rented out to someone, a stranger, someone who made me feel shy, someone with a booming voice, and I'd have to sleep on a fold-out bed on Moffa's floor. At seventeen I moved to the city, into a bedroom at the top of Annie the goth's house. She was a friend of someone's friend or a big sister or an aunt. Her house was cold and damp. Almost too empty and rough. I came back a month later and tried to show Moffa photos of rooms in the house with nice people in them, but nothing looked as interesting as those people and rooms felt, perhaps that's because nothing and no one was. The small bedroom I returned to was still full of boxes but had evidently been cleaned and made to look homely. Later I found out Moffa had rented the room to a man called Ali who drove a taxi and was sad to leave when I suddenly wanted to come back. At eighteen I left again for college, came back often throughout for no reason. Every time I had less and less to tell Moffa about where I'd been and what I'd done. I'd hardly moved on. So I shushed, retreated into corners and blankets. For a year or so I occupied Moffa's house quietly, without confidence. You need to have character to be audible. I used to make her jump. I would suddenly be right behind her in the lounge. She would scream, look at me, sigh, then go out for the night.

Moffa was weird in the way she dressed and spoke to herself, living in a world that I didn't feature in. Overall she seemed happy existing as if I did not—bursting into opera when I asked a question, always only making one cup of tea. My presence was too close to a bad dream that kept coming back. As soon as my silent moods got too much of an effort even for me, I left again, did a few things that got me more into debt, came back, left, signed up to another tenancy. I lived with a few men and women. Some were strangers who smelt funny in the morning, others were what people call partners, but that's not it. Someone sulky and just for a while. I trained to be a medical librarian while he trained to be a teacher. We shared a semi-fictional happiness in a greenish borough of a city. We did things like thoroughly researching and choosing some room colours for walls we were allowed to paint, that we stared at like penguins and that I'll never see again. I was with someone jolly but chronically ill, with someone who smoked and with someone who swam, all on and off for bits of an exorbitant but unfruitful decade. I've co-owned cooking utensils and DIY tools, bed linen, houseplants. I've desperately sought and subsequently desperately got rid of items of furniture. Who knows where it goes. I've cried over breakages of beautiful ceramics that I wouldn't care a fig about now if they were magically returned to me whole. I've lost bikes. I've worriedly cut bushes 'back.' I've tried to trick and tempt and triangulate work, love and their materials into an order. It never works. I was more myself living in the margin of Moffa's house. That is where I learned, like you, to lodge, I mean, adapt and hide my needs rather than dig down, simply hover without much substance, meekly occupy, as the tenant of the tenant, it's how I was born.

Moffa insomnia

Now I think about it, and I've thought about it a lot, there were ways I behaved living in the house with the mother and daughter that you're now in that were inappropriate. Behaviours that in combination with the jagged contrast of one person living with others made me a bad lodger. You can blame me for the fact that your landlady doesn't like sharing her space at weekends, likewise for the stain on the mattress. That was from a particularly induced bleed. From one Friday to Monday, all through the weekend, I bled heavily and painfully, lying in bed unwilling to move, going delirious, thinking about all sorts, about Moffa, about brown lipstick, my biting stomach, my failing the course, my being kicked in the stomach by every member of the class, about a chubby teenage boy raving inside me. I did not take any painkillers because I couldn't face leaving the house to buy some and having to re-enter the house again, risking having to have a conversation. Instead I lumped downstairs for the odd cup of sweet tea. It was the first weekend after the Christmas break. The presence of yet another needy and incapable body seriously fatigued the holiday-worn mother. But it was worse for me; I was sad to be so ill, inconvenient and alone, to bleed through the sheets and onto the mattress, to mark things that were out of my control, and all the time being aware that an event was happening to me that I couldn't focus on because I was embarrassed. While having to contain myself I was losing something; a small idea was travelling away from me, snagging on its way out. Whatever it was announced itself too quietly, the cramped and uncramped yearnings. The feeling was of multiple intrusions coming through and by way of me, a gargantuan smirk from fate, a deep out-of-place throb, have you felt it? I was gross at other times too: a revolting cold, food poisoning, a hangover so bad I was a dying star. I was so very in the way, a body is a torrent of impasses.

Before that Christmas I had gone through a naughty phase of visiting an Italian man who lived locally, in a house with tiger wallpaper. Luca was more like a thin boy, doing an anthropology PhD on human insecurity. We met on the bus travelling back from the college campus, where I did the course and where you are doing the course, and where he was having a meeting with his supervisors about food and violence. After moving my bag from the seat next to me I learned he lived in a house share two streets away from where I lodged, from where you lodge, so we made a date for me to go round. We had fun, I liked his smell, so started going over every week. Luca lived with a young couple, Lou and Ron, who were saving up and preparing to conceive a baby; who, despite having no sparkle of sexual energy between them whatsoever, wanted to continue the nothingness of their co-aura into the culture of a family. They both worked hard, long hours in a large hotel. There was once a fire in the hotel and it was an hour before Lou heard from Ron and even then it was hard to detect any fever for the other's existence. They were always tired and angry by the end of the day. They ate steaks with a packet sauce and jacket potatoes. They watched TV wearing loose-fitting clothes. On the fridge was a photo of them on their wedding day, wearing stiff white fabrics that sliced into their necks.

My weekly or twice-weekly knocks on the door, carrying a bag of wine to drink with their messy, unwanted and over-articulate housemate in the kitchen where they would have liked to sit as a family, where they had in their mind's eye a version of themselves happy, in love and duplicated, only to then have to listen to me shriek upstairs, being screwed by a sharply penised anthropologist while they watched a gruesome police drama—well it all must have been annoying. My trips in and out of the house late at night and early in the morning were trying on all sides. It meant clattering out of Lou and Ron's front door and back through my landlady's with the irritating audibility of someone drunk trying to be quiet. Funny how casual sex involves upsetting multiple sets of unrelated people. Life makes horrible door-whackers of us all.

At first my—our—landlady found the whole Luca affair

funny and exciting. She bombarded me with sisterly questions and giggles in the kitchen before I left for the tiger house the first few times. But by the time I had snuck in at 2 a.m. on a number of nights over the course of a month, and had once been sick noisily, under her roof, at dawn, my, our, landlady made it clear that my night trips to the Italian were inconvenient. Unhomely. I wasn't sure and I am still not sure. Who knows. I was done anyway, everything gets depressing. After only a few more times, then once more, then after a weekend away to a festival during which I saw a nasty car crash while he bumped into his young French ex-wife at a talk in a tent on radical architecture, I stopped. We have to roll into life and then quickly roll away from its hurts. But I'd offended the woman who housed me and it was a shame to have done that. I'd brought the habits of promiscuous sex, with its unsightly follow-ups, in proximity to where her preschool daughter slept. After that my relationship with her was less endeared. She still said, All right? to me in the morning, she said it sweetly and hurriedly in a way that enforced a boundary. Or was she just busy? All right, yeah, I'd say. And then begin to make a joke of myself but she'd dash away, carrying laundry or her child. I retreated into the margins again.

Did I have a choice to be less clumsy? No. Just as it is expensive to be poor, is it inevitable to be insensitive if you're a discomforted person? Yes. If you're unsettled, you're unsettling.

* * *

Are you lying awake? I was. Can you sleep? I couldn't. I wrote:

Dear Moffa
why can't I sleep here? And when I say *here* I mean at this age. Around the same as yours when you started having parties and disappearing. And when I say *here* you might have heard that I am back in town. My own place so don't worry about the bed in the small room. I'll drop by soon I still have my key for the back door. How are you? Also how am I so delicate and so rough? What happened to me? And what happened to you and why am I too nervous.
It's OK though it's all fine
I'll be triangle I mean tranquil I mean
I did the course
there's someone else there now
that's all there is to say
You starved me
there was nowhere to sleep I pretended to be a rabbit for one week
because it was easier to be a rabbit than a schoolgirl
I wanted to eat chicken
I'd like to go back now. Also
you forgot me and you filled our small house with people who

hounded me who ignored me who
no one fed me
and I want to say to you
I want to ask you

I live with Kav who I haven't heard come in yet
Kav is away and is half goat I
look like myself at the moment I look like a moth. A monthly.
A mouth.
I will be glad when this is over I will never send this

it is now a shopping list. Shampoo. Razors. Humous.

You meet more

Professor Dommer leaves money to keep his room vacant while he is away. Used to the extra occupant and always in need of a little more money, your landlady has made up an airbed for herself on her daughter's bedroom floor, freeing up her room for short lets. These are miniature lets really, only for one or two nights, sometimes a week. The first person to stay is a tall Mancunian woman in her early sixties called Bee who refers to the child as 'the little madam' and has a twitch on her left eyebrow. She plans to move into a housing co-op in a town closer to the sea and is waiting for her room to be vacated by someone who's been voted out. Bee wears long, flowing cardigans with huge pockets that bulge with tissues, pens, notebooks, sucky-sweets and lip balms. When she goes outside she wears a big hat and sunglasses. Bee spends most of her stay in the garden reading a glossy astronomy book. She likes to sit in the cool sun eating a tuna baguette, sometimes taking photos of galaxies with her phone, other times snoozing with the book and her eyes a little open. Bee is kind natured but something has gone terribly wrong in her life. Who knows what but it seems that a vital motor at the centre of her soul has collapsed. Wearing her sunglasses indoors and no longer capable of taking part in natural everyday conversations, she stands in her long cardigan in the busy kitchen, raising her voice over the extractor fan, talking to no one in particular, recounting incidental events that happened years ago, meditation retreats she's tried but found difficult, the odd time she's found herself homeless. The skin on her hands is red and irritated.

I wouldn't normally say this but we should avoid women like this. However kind they are, whatever wisdoms of experience they have, the catastrophe that happened to them might catch. We're vulnerable to their particular fate, one that would drag us in deep as if into a warm bed. That space in the corner of the room she stares into when she goes quiet begins as a safety, but follow her there and before you know it you are as alone as a pile of leaves. No one will know us. No one will know the song of our nature, where to contact us or what for. We'll stand in other people's kitchens unaware of how in the way we are. Let's just pull out our organs right now. When Bee is staying you make an effort to be kind and open, you follow her ramblings while the mother rushes around her daughter; you delay eating your crackers until there is a gap in her strange story, and even try to tell her about your course, encouraging her to enrol next

September. The details of the course seem to disturb some memory in Bee. She glares at a spot on your neck, calls it all a load of pretentious nonsense then ignores you. On the bedside table Bee leaves behind an old photograph of happy women in their forties, sitting on a moon-print sofa in a cramped living room, drinking wine and laughing. In the middle of them a young boy wearing sunglasses plays a small inflatable guitar, a woman who looks like a young Bee reaches to him. You try to get in touch to send the photo back to Bee but the phone number your landlady has for her goes nowhere.

Soon after Bee leaves a boy called Zed wearily arrives from Lagos. He needs somewhere to stay while the error in his university accommodation is solved. It takes five days. During his stay you sit on your bed together like teenagers, which he nearly still is, sharing music and watching videos, with the little girl nestled between you and sometimes jumping on your pillows. For your mutual entertainment you and Zed put headphones on the girl and each choose a song to play her. As soon as the music hits her ears the girl leaps up like a chemically altered mouse, bouncing off the bed onto the floor, and calling into the mirror, *I'm inside music*, shouting, *I am in songs*. Zed is about to do a fashion course but is already a kind of expert. He dresses you in outfits that you would never have dared or considered, matching clashing tops and skirts from the doldrums of your wardrobe, creating a stylish and brave version of you. Zed will sporadically message you pictures of fantastically dressed celebrities at galas for years after.

Now Gil is staying. Gil is a woman of everywhere, accent Greek and then French, veering to North American, her parentage is global ex-pat and ongoing. She is your age but much stronger and louder in everything: her coughs, her laughs, her steps. She is staying for three nights but her wailing stretches and her friendly tickles on your waist make it feel longer. Her life force is a forest. She occupies space in a way that makes everyone who falls into it feel lucid and comfortable. She is relaxed, released and untidy. Each night of Gil's stay has a theme: on the first night she teaches the child a dirty song involving the tits of a bear, a song with possible anti-Socialist undertones, but one she'd sung herself as a little girl with her brothers. On the second night she and your landlady get drunk in the garden and dance. You hear them from your bed while you are trying to read a textbook from your course's core reading list about triangulation of the self.

It is Gil's last night now and she'll leave for a nannying post in the morning. You are sitting side by side on the sofa. The child is sleeping upstairs and her mother is out with friends, having given in to Gil's insistent offer to babysit in exchange for a bottle of wine. At a nervy speed you have drunk most of it. You and Gil are learning about each other's lives through stories. You want to hear more of hers, which are exciting, unwinding tales compared with your synopsis of two house shares and a long-term relationship. Before coming here Gil had stayed with a family in Hanover, but had to leave in mild disgrace having slept with their 22-year-old—only recently returned from two years of backpacking—son. Gil says to you that she only wanted sex once but it was no good, I didn't come so we had to do it again the next day … I had unfinished business … but his father caught me running back to my room … in my underwear can you believe my luck? she asks. You laugh, a little aroused.

The scandal with the son meant Gil had to leave Hanover two months early, so she rejigged her year and came here, to soon take up a quickly arranged nanny job for wealthy professionals in a nearby village. While in the UK she wanted to: meet an amazing older lover, see a friend called Yaz again, save money to waste time somewhere else. Every half an hour she rolled a cigarette half-full with herbal tobacco and carried on the conversation from wherever she smoked. Damn Hanover boy, pretty eyes but no strength. I should've fucked the father, he was nice, or the mother eh!? Or maybe … You couldn't hear the rest. She calls to you from the garden, moving to the back door, then carries on calling to you while leaning towards the kitchen window, misfiring smoke all over the house. Gil returns to the sofa and looks at you, My sweet … I have an idea. She kicks her shoes off then reaches to you, takes your hands and presses down on your thumbs. We should rub each other's feet. You blush. Come on, she touches your leg, We'll never see each other again, I don't keep in touch. We have to mark this meeting with a ritual, it's beautiful. We need it eh? Come on, we're drunk, give me your legs … we'll do it properly.

When was the last time you were touched, you ask yourself. It's at least four months since your teenage niece rubbed your shoulders while her mother, your angry sister, hurriedly boiled a bag of stuffed pasta and shouted about her car. More recently there was a singularly bad and isolated hook-up that hardly counted as contact. Apart from that, the time since you had a lengthy platonic, or professionally endorsed, or sensually altering contact is in no uncertain terms long. Your body is private, so private even you have been cast out.

Without putting your wine glass down you flick your legs up onto the sofa to make a low-denier lattice with Gil's. You are dressed similarly to her in a skirt and blouse but she is filling space differently, her state is dazzling and familiar, she doesn't navigate, she sweeps her skirt, it's how she wears it. You drink. Another contrast is her well-proportioned leg that is magnificently heavy to hold in place as you sip once more, put your glass down on a book then go ahead, dig your knuckles into the balls of her feet and heels in imitation of what she is doing to you. Her left leg, your right. She pauses work on your toes to moan, squeezes them, then speaks ... You know ... it's beautiful to be us ... so in motion and full of pleasure ... we ... need to look after our feet. All the moving we do. You don't think? You look confused but I promise ... the accelerations in us are real ... we don't have to wait ... Take my parents for example ... my mother ... she is a hypocrite but also she is a genius ... well ... she followed my father around the globe while they were young ... had me and my brother as gifts for my father ... 'I have given you a sensible son and a beautiful daughter now buy me a house ... no more hotel suites, you bastard' ... my mother stayed by him and she stayed blonde ... three houses later in Singapore she was happy and she stopped bothering with my father ... seven years ago she got her first Shar Pei dog ... Apollo ... then Diego ... now she has twelve. Twelve Shar Peis! And she loves them ... her Shar Pei babies ... the old fat ones and the tiny wrinkly babies. I said Mom why so many Shar Peis!? She loves their folds ... She could spend all day neatening their skin like blankets ...

As she speaks Gil wraps her hand around your ankle and moves the flesh of your calves up and down, then starts bending your toes back. They click, you giggle. The relaxed smells from under your skirts mingle. It hurts how much she's bending your toes back.

... Look at me look at me please ... you worry about money ... ? C'mon! ... we should take our tights off ... roll yours down ... here let me ... no I mean it isn't what they think it is ... this you and me just by living ... it's more important to enjoy this than anything else you did today ... we have to be strong enough to enjoy luxuries ... Sometimes I cry when I am pressed here ... there ... it's a release of ... I'm going to clean your toes, you don't have to do mine but it's beautiful, like in the Gospels ... these wet cloths, they're soaked in essential oils ... from Cyprus ... you should have seen this shop o my god ...

With an exotic-smelling wet wipe Gil meticulously rubs between each of your toes, polishing the thin, tight webs of skin, scraping around and under your nails. You want to scream it tickles so much.

The dog of the house is resting his head on the seat next to Gil, gazing up at her. With no warning or indication of her next move she reaches off the sofa and takes out a piece of cured meat from her handbag. It looks like a long, dried purplish ear. Gil takes a bite of it and chews, then feeds the rest of the piece of meat to the dog, letting him lick her hand after the meat has gone so that his tongue turns the silver rings around on her fingers, then she moves her dog-licked hand back to your foot. She licks a finger on her other hand and moves it up your leg, still talking about the shop in Cyprus, how expensive the candles were.

* * *

A car rumbling outside your window stirs you, one hour since you boozily laid your body down on the bed. Something about the engine left running suggests a situation and wakes you up fully. You go to look, wobble at first, realising you got into bed naked and unwashed. You see a silver car below the house. Your landlady is sitting in the passenger seat, stiff and unspeaking. The street is dark and embarrassed. In the glow of the car the man in the driver's seat is animated, turned fully to her while she stares forward. The man rubs his face, laughing at his own speech. Without breaking her expression your landlady gets out of the car and passes under your view to enter the house. The car doesn't move, maintaining guard of her as she walks away. With the engine still on the man gets out and leans on the roof looking towards the house. He looks up. He sees you and you see him. Without hearing what they're saying you can tell your landlady is confiding in Gil, letting her into the secrets that twist through her life, telling Gil things she would never tell you. You lie back down in bed and listen to the two women's voices downstairs. They laugh and talk until the early morning. You hear them creep upstairs whispering so as not to wake you or the girl.

Moffa the walls

This is all so visible and obvious. It helps. I would like to rub your feet. I would like to sleep across the landing from you afterwards. I am someone who enjoys sleeping in bedrooms next to where other women are sleeping. Are you? There's a comforting logic in adjacency, isn't there?

For example the sounds that filtered through my sublet flat, coming from other people's front doors and living rooms, I fixated on them. I was pretty sure the upstairs neighbours had a fold-out bed. On the dot every evening at 10.30 p.m. there was a long squeak and then a satisfying clunk. Sometimes followed by a bang on my ceiling. This was a predictable regular sound and I liked it as a detail about people I knew nothing else about. Did the fold-out bed belong to someone who could no longer sleep in the same bed as their partner? Were they otherwise happy? Was it an extra person they were harbouring for money or kindness? They liked to watch *Question Time*, I knew that. The person whose front door is opposite mine was also endearingly regular, their slow—from either drunkenness or tiredness—steps to their front door yielded not much information except that they were a smallish person walking heavily, who banged doors. If I can picture the cause of the noise, if I can add a likeable characteristic or a sweet backstory, then it doesn't bother me. In fact the habitual commonness is homely. At completely irregular times I will be lying alone in a calm silence on my bed, looking at my phone, when I'll hear a cough, as clear and as loud as if it were my bedfellow's. That phantom cough has followed me to the places I've lived in all my life. And who hasn't sat at a desk by a wall writing something important or stressful one day only to realise that on the other side of that wall was someone's toilet? That sort of thing doesn't bother me any more.

Varying types of hard work have got me to the point of being able to say that. Before I found myself, before I started leaving Moffa, I used to be shy. Shyness is fear of being adjacent, which I fought my way out of by leaving the house and finding things I liked. Certain landmarks came before this though. There are days in a teenage girl's life that are like moments of restoration. In public or even alone, even sat next to a shouty father staring straight ahead and nodding while he discloses things we don't want to hear, we struggle but manage to return to a vibrant personality that was waiting for us.

I had a day like this lying on my bed at thirteen years old.

I was feeling shy even in the silence of what I thought was an empty house. Something in me was about to change. Do you know the Shangri-Las? The Sixties girl band made up of tragediennes from New York. They had a lead singer who sounded like a girl screaming out of her bedroom window across a fight in a car park. These tragediennes gave me the adjacency I've come to love: though I'm still shy sometimes, I think of them and feel like myself.

At the age of thirteen on this mellow Sunday I heard the Shangri-Las. Moffa's house had been silent all morning. I was lying on my narrow bed, trying to zone out in the patches of sunlight that dulled me and cooked the duvet cover. From nowhere a song by the Shangri-Las bellowed through the wall. I was trapped in my young stillness and didn't move as a loud American voice started insisting in a confident speaking tone, not singing, about being in love, and that I better believe it, and she spelled it out: L-U-V! I jumped. I thought the singer was there in the house! I didn't know anyone else was in, and they either didn't know or didn't care that I was there.

Pearl was playing the song. It's hard to remember why but for some reason there was a nineteen-year-old girl called Pearl staying in Moffa's bedroom and Moffa had gone away. When Moffa came back Pearl slept in my room and I slept on the floor. I wasn't easy to be around and even though Pearl was there to watch me during the week or two she stayed we barely talked. This was when I was shy. Triangleless. I wouldn't ask questions. Just say hello to people and move along, simply dressed in collared T-shirts and avoiding Moffa's perfume for dear life. This nineteen-year-old Pearl was quite shy herself. Or perhaps she didn't like me.

Don't you think it's a strange song to play in someone else's house? Loudly in the morning? Would you? If I was in her situation I would not. But she did. A song which is mostly a melodramatic conversation between the teenage girls about a boy one of them *luurvs*. In their soapy voices the girls go through the boy's potential factors, going up and down him, this boy, with wavy hair that's a little too long, who's bad in a good way, and not evil, and all of it spoken in a forlorn dialogue, so intimate and close, sounding so shocking to me in a quiet house with two people in separate rooms not talking. It rang strange, and felt like an invitation to not be shy, to not fear being on one side of the wall.

When the song finished I heard the girl walk over to her CD player and put it on again. I lay still and listened with her, all the way through then all the way through again. Was she thinking about someone? Feeling them and missing them and really thinking about them in the percussive chorus that talks about walking right up to the boy, like the singer is going to kick the poor guy and rob him, but actually kiss him, give him a great big kiss, a sweet but targeted one without tongues. Through the wall the floor creaked, I heard it, Pearl was dancing and singing along, then Moffa's bed puffed as she jumped on it. That boastful life leaked through the wall, a nineteen-year-old's first thrill of wanting someone, so much, without shame. Overhearing it happen gave me my triangulation of the self: the sex, the fun, the plastic trousers in the age of rocket ships. The song is somewhere to go. That song is a one-woman feeling. Teenage girl desire is a kind of packaging but anyone can get in on it, and return to it. The Shangri-Las click their fingers to girls turning into women on the ticket of wanting. If you're allowed to mature that way without trauma—and did you?—the song sings to you. The young girl in our heart snacking compulsively on her treat of love never leaves us. What a song to play in someone else's quiet little house! When they go, really? You go, Yes! And when they go, how? You go, Close! And when you want to go, you go higher and happier, you go bah-boom bah-boom bah-boom, along with racy drumming, and your friends go too. We all go wild, we all bang on the wall. Having our hearts out. Have a strange day, strange girl. Strange Pearl. ('The Pearl' is the name of one of my massage techniques.)

* * *

Triangles

Triangulation in the family occurs when one parent negates the selfhood of a single child by treating a sibling with explicitly more or less care, or by using the child as a device in their relationship with another parent, or by creating a situation with another figure in the household that isolates the child completely. The child will then mature without differentiation of the self. (And we don't want that, do we?) These are examples of pathogenic parenting, but you can see versions of it in all households.

Triangulation in the workplace involves one or both persons in a conflict manipulating or drawing a third person into the dynamic to create another conflict, thus reinforcing their power. Narcissists do this to gain attention for themselves, but it can also be practised lovingly with the goal of deflecting tension.

In geometry, triangulation is the process of measuring

the distance from two known points to a third point. You work out where something is by its relation to other things. It's about coordination—it's a kind of localisation.

In data science, triangulation is when you analyse the same findings three different ways to test the hypothesis. It's a process of rigour and caring about truth.

What I learned on my course took elements from all of these theories—adding some Buddhist principles of the three bodies, bits of acupuncture and some dance. The truth is, in any form of philosophy, mysticism, alternative medicine, science or psychology you can't move for triangles. The triangle is the end point, the goal of being. Doing triangles is inevitable, triangulating money–housing–sex, work–family–art, father–son–holy ghost. Coordinate yourself! the teacher said, Triangulate, riddle treat-trauma, send the past somewhere else. Massage someone to create a triangle.

You agree to the George

The professor is back and he wants to take you out for a drink one evening to the local pub, which you agree to and I don't want you to feel bad, I would have done it too, and have, because some thirsts, and the polite formalities that bring us into contact with them, are homely. The question is asked in a way that feels like more of a recap of a previous arrangement. He uses the word 'should' like going for a drink together is a task that needs ticking off a list. And it is, isn't it? It's obvious. He says, We should go for a drink tonight. There's a seminar I need to be around for tomorrow … and then Friday I'm … He trails off, reading an email on his phone. Is this how husbands and wives talk over breakfast? The slice of toast in his hand is drooping, the spoon of muesli in your hand has slightly missed your mouth. You say, Uh huh, sure, and wipe milk from your chin while reading about a rescued mountain climber on your phone.

Sure let's go ... to the pub? There is a pause while he chews his toast crust. The George? Yes. Or Amelie's? O, I don't mind. You let the question hang. Let's go to the George, he says and then, Goodbye moppet, to the girl sitting opposite you, who is eating her cereal and has been humming loudly throughout your conversation. You wonder to yourself, Is this how it feels to be a family?

Why does he lick himself there?

What?

Pluto, look.

O, that's just how dogs are.

* * *

Heading straight from college after an evening class, you arrive at the pub just before seven, find a table in the corner with a good view of the large TV that's showing a muted singing contest. Sip at your small white wine and wait. After fifteen minutes of rationed sipping you hear a familiar throat clearing and realise the professor is already here at a table behind you staring into his phone, his glasses on his forehead and slipping down onto his nose. Here you are, he says as you approach and laughs for no good reason. Out of the context of the house he looks different, less announced, more like a doctor. In this unfamiliar pub his paunch is an object that you know and feel warm towards, as you do towards a friend in a crowd or when you see a fox in the street at night.

He's already bought you a large red wine so that's two drinks to drink quite quickly; that's an instant toxin flush and a bad night's sleep; that's quite annoying actually. He points at it, I've seen you drink those. That is not true. You rest your elbows on the table. Keeping your bag on the empty seat between you suggests you are working something out about this situation. The professor scratches his head, messing up hair which at once makes him more attractive. Why is that? He is trying and retrying a joke about the furniture in the pub, you think. The professor has a daughter who lives in Australia and who he suggests must be nearly as old as you but that cannot be right. As he talks about her your shoulders rise and fall, your legs squeeze and loosen. Your wool skirt itches. You follow the flick of his shirt collar from his jobbish body back to the reality of his voice. What is he saying? Have your hand on the glass stem on the table. Now he is miming the handling of some rare brain-scanning machinery he used at a lab in Utrecht, but you missed the beginning of his story so have to guess if what he is saying is shocking, impressive or amusing. Every table around the pub seems populated by people who exist to fabricate this scene of you having a drink with a professor. The boys playing pool, the local Labour party members having a meeting, the three people in trek wear are somehow only there to make you on a date with the professor plausible and real.

I would relax and allow myself to flirt if I were you. My problem is I'm always falling for these moments, I always move the bag. I would let the pub wine go right into my adrenal gland then tally up my hot pangs one by one. I would open the ways and close the ways in equal measure, chase the triangle, find the triangle. But you're just laughing, now you understand what he's saying about the machine; it sounds like pigs, it feels like a car wash. You're genuinely laughing because something he said was funny for a second. Could the professor be an imaginary daddy? He found his way into the house without awareness or a plan, because he doesn't need one. No, what he is saying is not funny any more, his research into selective amnesia and how to implement it is *pioneering*. His daughter is starting out in the same field but more on the hypnosis side, She's more witchy. Hahaha. Yeah. The professor talks about his daughter a lot and whenever he does his voice moves a note until he's almost a father in a musical. He insists on her cleverness interspersed with small descriptions of what she looks like. Her hair was so long all her life, now she's cut it all off! She's a runner. She loves getting her way. Top marks all the way through school and still doing so well. Gets her long legs from her mother. Finds Sydney really forward-thinking. Could it be that he wants to make you jealous of her success and his caring admiration of her? What is he putting on display? I can't imagine loving this man, not even as his daughter. You can. You're sad. You want to replace his daughter. That's when you move the bag so there is nothing between you.

I like this pub, you say. That is a nothing statement that stands in for admitting you're nearly having a nice time so you must mean it as well as wanting to change the subject. Neither of you once mention the house where you both live at the moment or the child that lives there too, who you've both prepared after-bath supper for (one slice of Marmite on toast and a bowl of Rice Krispies with a plastic cup of very milky tea), or the mother who is always in another room rushing to do something out of view, something like ripping the hairs out of a woman's upper thighs or from a man's back, or washing her child and feeding her, or vacuuming a bedroom. Instead you talk about the comfort of beds in the abstract, hardness and softness, your varying need for sleep.

Trying to explain your course derails the conversation. You say, it's like osteopathy but more folk, like reiki but stronger. Experimental and traditional. There's lots of theory to get your head around. There's all sorts of directions you could take it in afterwards: sports massage, counselling, occupational hyper-remediation. I'd have to retrain, or make my training more specific, this course is very open to interpretation. You blush talking about yourself and drink quicker. He gazes curiously at you and after a pause says, Yes of course. You'd both prefer the conversation to pass back to him where there's more script. So he can say things and you can hold yourself listening. You drink a little more until the professor announces that he wants to test your memory. He lists over thirty household objects, which you can't remember, and asks you to repeat them back, which you cannot. Now listen, he says and leans in, he holds your gaze, he says, The mop touches the bucket, the bucket caresses the broom, the broom strokes the … He talks to you in a curiously romantic way about each of the objects. He lists them again and you remember every single one in order, drunk as you are.

Moffa the wardrobe

In life we briefly get to say the truth ourselves. The rest is admin and apologising. How clothes fit at first is a lie that becomes true. Since I arrived back here in my hometown I have been wearing the same acrylic top: a black scratchy jumper with machine-ribbed rows that catch my loose hairs. When wearing it I sweat yet I don't feel warm, just wet and weighed down. Still, I keep picking it up and putting it on. It gets covered in bits. I didn't buy it, no idea where it came from. I need to stop wearing it, I hate the feeling of it. If Kav walked into the room now I would appear to be someone who owns and likes to wear this jumper. That's how Kav would know me. And Kav could walk into the room at any moment. I'd have to say, O don't mind me, I haven't unpacked yet, I need to go clothes shopping. I don't know what Kav would do. Sniff me and neigh? I will buy more clothes tomorrow. I will tell Moffa I am

lunchbox snacks to steal, then return to the sofa with a sigh and chew into the night. But you can't relax and enjoy being alone because you're with the professor, laughing at the toys that look like they're having a meeting. The professor interprets your laughing as a wild display of abandon. He laughs too but he doesn't know why, using laughter as a channel to approach you. There is a brief exchange of energies, some pathways open. You look up at him and pass him your shoes. He takes them and says something about a nightcap as he strides into the kitchen, opening and closing cupboards without being quiet enough. I'm not stealing her drink, you say. The surprise curtness in your voice freezes the mood. The professor goes quiet and comes back to you from the kitchen. No, he says a little wounded, of course I wasn't going to *steal* anything. You realise he's holding a bottle of greenish schnapps that Gil must have left. You sit together on the sofa and swig from the bottle. The strong sugary liquor makes your head and stomach churn. What if you were sick on him? He'd know what to do, he's had kids. The conversation must have lost its spark because you're imagining vomit. The accusatory sound in your voice saying 'steal' is hanging in the atmosphere. The professor can't seem to move on from it. For some reason he starts telling you how much his grants are worth. Two million pounds is a lot of money. How much of that do you get? That's not how it works. No, sorry, you say, and remember Gil's legs on the sofa. He says something about the landscape changing. You say, Yes the landscape is always changing. There's a pause. He says, Busy day tomorrow.

This statement shifts into a confession about how stressful his work is, how much he misses his daughter and how he just wants to take some time out. There's a long pause. You look at him but there is only a small light on and you don't have your glasses, plus you're drunk, so he appears murky and semi-real, like a beige fire. In a moment like this where you can't make out the social features of a face, you can say anything. You consider sitting on his lap. Biting his ear. Even better, leaving this long pause and not saying a word. Your shoes have joined the meeting. You laugh, he laughs, you stand up, he stands up, you say goodnight but he doesn't move out of your way. You'll have to move past him so you might as well experiment, press into him for just a second. When you get to bed, I wonder, do you chase the triangle? Open up all the ways then shut them. Hiccup, race the grids, sleep.

Moffa the night

Open to the devastation of not sleeping, I gave up on my bed and lay down on the cola-stained sofa. Did I hear the hooves of Kav while I slept? If I became too lonely, could I have summoned Kav? I drifted. Some faces poked through my unconscious and talked me out of sleep. Instead I started remembering things; I put past thoughts in my head and spun them, they found each other and reacted, like I was electrocuting myself with memories. Once I'd gone over the worst of them I couldn't think of anything reassuring. Nice views are impossible to refind when you're lost, birthday parties are similarly difficult to picture apart from the final reflection in the mirror at the end of the night.

I focused on the voice and actions of the sweet girl I used to live with, along with her mother, in a house that had a constant thick heat and clean double glazing. I wanted to be closer to them but couldn't find a way in. Something about my time there wouldn't unwind itself and disappear like all the other places I'd lived: that mother, her daughter with the same long eyelashes. I played over the last look my landlady gave me, like she couldn't trust anyone, like however well she was carrying everything and however strong she felt, something or someone would cause her to drop everything, and it could be anyone at any moment, anyone she met, anyone who arrived at her door unannounced. To defend herself she'd call everyone babe and be more beautiful than them. She had to invite them in, including the one who'd break her.

All I had to do was play myself in my thoughts, with subtle differences. Push my shame out. Put my fantasies in the middle. Get them confused. Reorder my successes and decisions. I could see you lodging. You were in your first term. We'd both need to redecide what to do next September. Let's not get too confused by this year. An in-between one, I'd call it. If it got too disorientating I could stare at Moffa's house and understand where I was. I went to her house again. There was always something to watch on TV and half-sleep to. I didn't see Moffa on the TV again but I knew she might be there if I looked through all the channels one by one then back through them again.

I wondered for the first time where she might actually be. Was she still in plays? She used to play such untouchable and histrionic characters. They terrified me. Big women with loud, diverging voices; Amandas, Phèdres, Medeas, Lady etceteras. Did she still move around the country sleeping in obscure houses? Did she still arrive in musty bedrooms and open her suitcase with a Ha! like she'd never in her life seen any of the things she'd packed inside it? Did she snort at her nightie as she refolded it then set a small photo of her own mother dressed as a goddess by her bed? It would not have surprised me if she did, eating huge takeaways with a cider. Did she still get drunk with the technicians, still sleep with the ones who called her Queenie? Did she remember leaving me for weeks or, even worse, dragging me with her? Driving all the way to Newcastle? My sulk and her excitement lasting as long as the motorways. I did not have any good feelings about her car.

You clutch

What was so funny in the night? Your toys made me laugh. There is laughing in your bedroom, the girl is angrily holding the ballerina. Your toys were *still* making me laugh, they're even making me laugh now, I can't stop laughing … She pushes you, Stop laughing! You drop to the floor and roll around, clutching your belly, Ho ho ho. She leaps on top of you, batters your chest, puts her head underneath your blouse and screams. Ho ho ho. With a nimble burst of knuckles and punches, she mistreats the event, jumps up and lands on you again. Ow ow ow. Ho ho ho. Everything between you for the moment is cute and barbaric, detached from any scale of the maternal. That's why it's so fun. She kicks you. This is when we see what a child really is—right at the point of having no idea what a child is. From a distance in close contact, when she's not your responsibility exactly, but a care you've taken to be brash with, we play-wrestle and observe: a child is a moving bloom of orphaned licence. Her world is made of unstoppable radial prompts. A child moves as she thinks, the two are the same, and because she cannot understand who you are, she bangs into you. You do the same when you can't understand what your life is, you bang into things. In turn you realise where your body goes when you're around children and how it attempts to be symbolic but fails, like a bounced cheque, so full of its business at the outset, seeking permanence, but going nowhere.

The play fight ends with her sneezing on you before jumping up to run to the dog that's been worriedly barking at the disorder on the carpet. When she reaches the dog she sneezes again, the dog barks, she screeches, the dog howls. Then into the kitchen, where there's a clattering sound that must be cereal boxes being knocked down off the shelf. With the waft of a shower smell the professor comes out of the downstairs bathroom to find you on the floor, smiling and alone. He smiles back at you like you've been placed there for him. Good morning, you messaged me? Really, what did I say? Just the word, Tri. O sorry it was an accident. I see, he says, then loafs into the kitchen to claim the scene and make jokes with the child.

Moffa the view

Your time lying on the carpet may well have overlapped with my time standing there at the window in my sublet flat, sucking a lozenge. It'd been how long? A month or over. On the third floor of a block of flats that I remembered being built about twenty-five years ago as part of a wave of bizarrely placed housing developments. Its two well-placed windows in the main living space took in some good light but did not overlook Moffa's house. Did I mention that? From the bedroom window, when I stood on the bed, I could see some of her house, enough to conjure an image of her in action. I could imagine how she was faring in that small house. Not much happened in my mental pictures of her except for her wandering outside every now and then to lug things around the patio then lie down on a stack of old tyres, smacking her lips at the sky and humming, then falling asleep in the sun. On weekdays a delivery van often went up her street, I saw multiple attempts to deliver her parcels. A postman knocked when I was in there once but I ignored it. The nice neighbours took it.

The neighbours who wanted us gone all those years ago had now gone themselves. Their houses looked lighter, with blinds instead of net curtains, and jazzy numbers on the door. I could still see the old neighbours' faces. I had turned their faces into a massage of light energy strokes. Moffa had long outlived the gossip from those days, the complaint-excretions of the old neighbours, the words that embarrassed me so much. The reek of scandal that I stepped back into whenever I returned. And I kept coming back. For her everything was normal. But I kept returning to the same point. I just wanted a bath but couldn't bring myself to have one. As soon as I saw her I remembered what they called her. She just sang and bought lamps.

The new neighbours were two youngish families who I'd heard liked Moffa very much. The teenage children probably banged on her window and waved to her as she watched telly on their way to meet friends on the corner. I looked at the small flat around me. Still no sign of Kav. I stood like a statue. Still no sign of Kav. I made a cup of tea. Still no Kav.

You barbecue

Like a tin pencil case your intimate life is snapped shut and put away during your lodging hours. I imagine that you think to yourself, there's no time or place for me to express myself. All that is about to change.

The deal is you are not around at the weekends. This was always the arrangement, one that you eagerly agreed to, as much of a pain as it is to be constantly moving. On weekends you sometimes go back to the city to stay with your friend Ann Yosy. You have an arrangement, or rather a habit, and are welcomed most of the time. If you can't afford the train or Ann Yosy is away, and a room in her house isn't available to you, you might stay in your lodgings but be out all day, go on a day trip to a local village or seaside or something. A day trip, dear God. Ah the medieval state of mind, forts, o the ruins of empire, piers. How interesting. That you keep out of the way and stay busy is the main thing. The weekend of the house is not for you. Precious time. Your life will contaminate it. Every week, whatever inclination you start to have to stay and enjoy the warmth and the easiness of the clean, open-plan, L-shaped warm space, your departure is stressed by enthusiastic questions about your plans for Saturday and comments about how relieved you must be to get away from 'this mad house' to have a nice relaxing Sunday. You don't remember ever relaxing on a Sunday. You are fascinated by weekends and what is supposed to be done on them. How do people relax other than sleep, and when is the proper time to do that other than when it simply can't be helped? But this weekend is different. Through a mix of misfired politeness, diverted self-awareness and a child's big mouth you've hung around for a barbecue.

As far as I can recall a barbecue is a gathering of women with plates—hundreds of plates—while more children than you feel comfortable with run around in the garden. There are yet more plates, and then extra children with cheerful mixtures of clothing come around the side of the house, through the gate, until 2 p.m., when it starts getting noisy. Loud pop music that doesn't make sense and belonging to the taste of either the children or the mothers plays continuously. After eating, the children start sweating and crying, the women drink glasses of fruity alcohol and talk about needing to 'leave soon' for around three hours until finally, as the sun sets, the last of the women walk away or are collected by a car. I expect this barbecue will go like so and end as they tend to do.

It is undeniably autumn now but still mild and there's a bright enough sun to heat a group of people on some decking. Women greet each other in the kitchen with laughing hugs and kisses. You, like me, awkwardly drink the sparkling wine offered. Unlike me, you carry plates of burgers into the garden and place them on a fold-out table. You snap out the bread buns and pile them up as a woman who smells strongly and deliciously of vanilla arranges sauces, all the sauces: ketchup, mayonnaise, barbecue sauce, mustard, garlic mayonnaise, hot sauce, tomato relish, a blue cheese sauce. You put a handful of spoons in a jug and hope it's right. You pour crisps into a bowl and shuffle it around on a table without space until someone called Naomi says, Here love, and takes it from you. She splits the taut cellophane covering a glass bowl of heavily mayonnaised pasta salad with confident and swift piercing. Another woman has brought a tiny grey dog with her. The dog is called Whisky, it yaps and growls at Pluto, who takes to his basket. All the women move quickly, bracelets and nails clink against plastic. You hum as you slowly saw a baguette into medallions. They will begin to ask you what you do but what they really mean is, Who are you? and, What you are doing here? My course is pretty hard but very interesting, you answer, It's going well, I got a loan. You smile and look at the children as you talk to make clear your link to the family, but it isn't convincing. The children laugh and play with no interest in you. The girl you live with is being snooty to impress her friends. It's so lovely you could stay, you are told by your landlady's mother, who doesn't look that much older than her, as if it's a question. She has a slanting bob of bleached hair that makes her look controlling. It's so lovely to be here, you reply. The girl runs past you and you reach out to casually stroke her ponytail but she dodges you and you miss. After everyone has finished asking you questions about your course and stopped talking to you altogether they start new conversations about their children and the local school they all attend. The grandmother goes inside to do continuous small chores in the kitchen while the mothers sit in a circle near the barbecue under fleece blankets, stroking their own arms and passing salad. The titular barbecue is turned on by a switch and gradually heats a selection of burgers, sausages, halloumi, peppers, sauce-pasted mushrooms and sticky chicken drumsticks.

Between the mothers there are shared jokes about the school's designated odd kids, including one very odd kid, such an odd kid he gives them the creeps. Odd kid, they say. The private lives of their own children are discussed as openly as if they were not playing a metre away. Your landlady talks about her daughter's new interest in death, which you didn't know about. It is then learned that a boy with an adorable ponytail, you look at him, has been struggling to bond with the mother's new boyfriend until just this week, when Mo, the boyfriend, a younger man, consoled the boy over the loss of his grandad. The mothers adore this story, which has clearly been an ongoing and evolving narrative. Mo, you infer, is a shy man, but also gentle and model good-looking. One woman states that she wouldn't mind being consoled by Mo. Another woman gestures to her child, a four-year-old girl who is the youngest here, and who is obsessed with kissing her older half-brother: day and night she goes for him, draws pictures of them kissing, makes up songs about it, they have to guard the toilet door. This seems to half amuse, half deeply worry the mother but it doesn't register as a problem with the rest of the group. Similar stories are used to reassure her that it's a phase. In fact there is a lot of reassuring talk, that is the main pleasure of their speech. But there's more, apparently the girl does all sorts of things to the cat and cannot be looked away from for a second after she shits. You look at the tiny girl in question as her elders go over her perversions. She is dancing at the edge of the garden in a corduroy skirt with thick blue tights and a purple jumper, picking carefully selected leaves off a bush then stopping to applaud a much older girl, maybe eight, who is doing a handstand, and shouting, Sore grey! It must be a phrase she has picked up from repeated adult encouragement: That's sore grey, your doin sore grey. She points at her mother, Haha mummy your sore grey! She seems like a nice kid, also odd. All the kids seem like odd kids, odd and nice. Someone asks, Do you have children? No, not even an imaginary one. That was a weird reply. No one is to blame, conversations are hard with you. What can anyone say to you; Do you worry about money? What do you believe in? Your course is all there is and you can't talk about it any more than you have; in order to fully understand the course you'd have to actually do the course. Do you use products on your hair? It's really shiny.

So this is a Sunday. How does it feel? Life is a motion

of square blocks that recede from birth, collecting habits. Life is less interesting than hair dye. The afternoon goes slowly, delivered in rounds of meat, a little childhood weeping, lemonade spills, dropped sausages and sprayed ketchup. The sun peaks at 3ish when it suddenly feels like summer again. Blankets are let to fall off bare shoulders then collected by children who roll themselves up in them and around on the ground. A podgy boy who rolled into your chair looks up at you with a worried face. The conversation circles everyone's life then takes notice of you again.

She went on a date with the professor! your landlady announces to her friends, because dates are fun and interesting and good for conversation. Everyone looks at you. They want to hear more and ask what he looks like. You say, Not really a date, just a drink. He looks like a man with glasses who's about fifty-three. Your landlady says, O he's so sweet. She is giving you attention at last and you don't want it, the focus is wrong. I would hate this. He's so sweet though, isn't he? Like a big teddy, always happy, he makes himself a cheese sandwich every day. Aww, they say, Do you like him? You remain as silent as you can on the matter and smile painfully, picturing his damp nose. His thumbs. You turn the questions back on your landlady and ask where she stayed out so late the other night, Did you have a good time? you ask, affecting their feminine teasing, at which everyone goes quiet and looks into their drink. There's a sting in the air until the woman who brought Whisky the dog changes the subject entirely to an absent friend who is in hospital having hard tissue removed from a scar. From then on, as awkward as you are, you are truly out of the conversation. What would I do? I would drink more cheap sparkling wine and relax into the protein of a warm autumn sun and my unrelinquished blanket.

You feel the need to functionalise your idle presence by charming the children. As we have seen, however, it is one of those days, and I get them too, when you are without charm. The children take no notice of you or your nice questions about their superhero clothes. Two children dressed as Spider-Man are burping competitively, getting bolder until a guff of barbecue chicken and orangeade reaches you. I would give up on the children if I were you, I'd sit myself down next to one of the mums and start laughing at anything she says, flick my hair around and point my empty glass at the moving wine bottle. But you labour on with the children. What can you do to win your young friend's attention? She is one of six children now, which is more like a mass, a significance of garden matter that shrieks at its own worms. You really should give up. Fake an intriguing life problem (not one of your real ones) and get some tough-love reassurance from the mums. Who wouldn't want that? To look at painted fingernails? To be in the circle?

The girl does eventually notice you as you hover near her. Who is that lady? a little friend of hers asks. People speak to me like that too. The girl takes your hand and presents you to her people. You are introduced in boastful words you don't fully understand—they must be strange mutations of the word 'lodger'—until eventually the girl breaks into a dance, offering her main demonstration of who you are: Not Pretty! It catches on shockingly quickly: the small rave-like dance moves and the repeated chant, the little arrowed fingers pointing at you. I agree you had no choice but to join in with this, and you do a fine job, almost too good, of meeting their roughness with roughness, by tickling the first child to say it each time. You get hot and take off your sweater, really flinging yourself into the role of ogress, snarling and pretending to bite their hands, putting your sweater over a child's head. Two children's heads at once. An over-excited girl screeches so loudly at you, NOT PRETTY, that you dive on the ground as if you'd been shot. I think that was a mistake, but it's what you seem to do when lost for your next move, you fall to the ground. All hell breaks loose on you. You are drummed, you are laughed into and laid on, handfuls of grass are ripped up from the lawn and piled on your head. Not Pretty! rings in your ears. Maybe your shoes are taken off. A boy who was rhythmically kicking your buttocks catches the girl's face as she is sprawled on your back. It hurts her. You can hear her crying into your ear but can't move and have to try and comfort her with phrases that go into the soil. Her crying accelerates, the chanting doesn't stop.

I ask myself in these moments, who disappears? When we cannot see anything, who is it that is gone? I believe we share this maladapted conception of presence. We share it with each other and with babies. Also chimps. As when a baby covers its eyes and believes it has vanished, we likewise feel ourselves gone and elsewhere. Just from looking away, we transcend into a new state, one disparate and rented. When we're alone in a room, it's not that no one is with us, it's that we are with no one. I'm not sure where I am now but I know I'm not there. Go on then, fall into the phrase and back through your thoughts. This is when I look at you.

When you finally stand up from the pile of children you feel a little odd. Something is not right in the world; you're not injured but a vital ordinariness is missing. Three of the children are pointing and laughing at you, the rest have run away screaming. There's something not right about you. You look down and see one of your breasts is peeking out from your bralette and vest. What a sight. Mole-ish, looming out of the side, mostly cotton-covered but nosing into the exterior world without scepticism. It is a paltry transgression, I wouldn't worry about it. The grandma has come to cuddle and carry the girl, who is still crying and looking at you unusually, away. The grandma, however, manages to show disapproval with no obvious acknowledgement of your bad state. You gather yourself in and brush yourself off as the rest of the children disperse, instantly forgetting you. The mothers didn't notice a thing. Children's screams are one long life-noise to them.

In an attempt to be casual you pick up one of the cold burgers and a stiff half of pita bread (you have not, we might do well to remember, eaten anything yet) and assemble them. The grandma is waving wet wipes at you from the kitchen. Would you like to come in and clean up? she calls. It is a curiously calm power women like this have, I've felt it a few times, it's like being near a statue of a monarch. We have to go to them when they wave at us. The grandma is a woman who plays badminton competitively. You take a bite of your burger in a pita and walk into the house through the French windows. It's been lovely of you to join us, she says, Thank you for staying a little while, I'm sure you've got places to go now. She does more of the washing up and looks out of the window. She tells you that 'the girls' hardly ever get to see each other like this these days, they're so busy with the children. Yes, you say, through burger, it's been lovely. You leave a long pause then you add, But I should be getting going now. Yes, she says, washing up, thank you again for helping. You leave the house holding pita bread.

With nowhere to go you make your way to a newsagent's to buy a can of beer. The shop feels normal and homely with only two other customers stood in a line. They are quiet and alone needing ham and newspapers. You take the beer to walk in a circle around the local park where a crowd of teenagers are one by one practising their screams. Their sound will later be replaced by similar ones from foxes. You turn into the wooded area to wee. A dog walker happens upon you squatting by a tree and you both laugh through it. I needed a wee, you say, I'm just walking my dog, she says, then you carry on with your businesses. You message Ann Yosy to see if you can go there but don't hear back. So you circle the park. After about an hour of walking and sitting on benches I would agree that it is safe to go back. As you approach the house you see your landlady sitting on the front doorstep catching the last of the shifted-around sun catching her chest in the space between the blanket over her shoulders. Her daughter is next to her, skipping up and down the step drinking a bright pink drink, but somehow kept steady by her distantly gazing mother. Together they are slurping and illuminated, living a quiet wholeness without you. That world is burst when you step onto the drive and kick the dish of cat food. The girl gasps, her mother blinks and refocuses as if she cannot remember who you are.

Moffa the neighbours

Shame is a kind of energy. We know this because of the course. Shall I share my shame-image? My finest work?

The neighbours came to Moffa's house when I was eleven or that kind of young, at that kind of time. They were dressed up in small-town business clothes with ugly shoes and wanted to do a citizen's eviction on us. Moffa wasn't in or was in her bedroom not answering the door, my memory is jagged. It was me alone, holding a magazine and my cat before she'd run away. As they spoke a ginger tail and gossip pages dangled at my knees. You live like pigs! they shouted as soon as I opened the door, before it was open, then as the door was still opening, as my cat wriggled to escape into the road. They said something about breaking tenancy laws that they'll be telling our landlord about, All the people, all the disgusting weirdos coming in and out. It was two women, who looked like they were composed of lilac nylon and hatred, plus one man, slower, with eyes straight ahead, staring at nothing. I think I said, Sorry, as one of the two windswept women's faces briefly uncoiled in acknowledgement that it was me, the creepy child, they were performing their near-erotically charged intervention on. Is she here? she asked, and her lips went like a set of pink drawers sliding in and out. Why aren't you at school? I said, Easter, or I thought, Easter, and I saw a lamb, running. My eyes filled with tears. It must have been one of their husbands standing silently behind them, his large head held in place by grey sideburns. I looked at his nose to stop myself crying because his hairy nostrils were so wide and unusual to me.

It was a memory that maladjusted in scale as I matured, remaining a gross vision of melting faces. It blurred with my memory of Moffa's parties and wild nights, cigarettes stubbed into cheese, life upside down with a draught running through the house because the front door had fallen open. I didn't know the word 'mayhem' then, just that the draught was cold, and that I had a headache, possibly my first-ever headache, and from then on I thought headaches were caused by unshakeable mental images of distorted adults, like these spiteful faces curving through the door and yelling: This is a citizen's eviction, your mother, said one of them, Is a tart, said another, Your mother, said the original, needs to pack up. I wanted to cry but instead considered my wrists sticking to cat hair and magazine pages. The husband made a grunting noise in agreement. I politely stood aside so they could call past me to where

Moffa might have been, You live like PIGS! This child is neglected. A finger pointed at me as I held the door open for them, for as long as they needed to say their piece. I think it repeated a few times. Or that was how the memory encoded; rewound and replayed with aggressions in the layers of seconds, of minutes, while I leaned on the radiator and wanted nothing but to read my magazine and let the cat go. I held the door. I turned to look up the stairs in the direction of the shouting and to where the man was channelling his masculinity. I don't remember what happened next. Did Moffa come down or call me away? Did we all get sucked into my massive, non-responsive awkwardness until I apologetically shut the door and thought, Easter. Does time recycle itself? Does a lamb enjoy what it knows? Do front doors really only open and close?

The neighbours kept a couple of horses in an illegal field behind the houses. A mare and her offspring with cracked shins surrounded by dandelions; they were anonymously reported as being malnourished and bruised. Someone within Moffa's network of allies had sorted it all out, got the horse-abusing-would-be-bailiff-neighbours prosecuted and threatened with more. And that was that. There was always someone who wanted Moffa around more than those who wanted her gone. She was like a beautiful local prize to some people, and an error that needed correcting to others. What a sad, mean decade to cast Moffa as a pariah, because she had little parties and gave shelter to people like Ali and Pearl, as well as the others, Kamil, Denny, Aka and Dean. Charging just enough for rent and wine. Breadsticks and electricity. Dangly earrings and cat food! Olives. Toilet roll. Shampoo.

But no one told me about the horses or the smoothing over. So I grew up in worry, I doubled it up and plied the word tart to a turning out. What they called her. Would they come back? I managed it into a therapeutic move.

You answer the phone

The phone is ringing and you are alone in the house. The mother and child have gone swimming, expected back at seven, smelling nice. The TV is boring, you are slurping peppermint tea, ignoring the phone appropriately. If there was something good to watch you wouldn't want to answer the phone.

Hello?

It's me.

A man's voice. One that fills you like hot tea.

I'm not …

O. It's not you?

Yes.

Who is this then?

Say, I'm a lodger, or say, It's *the* lodger. It's easy.

I'm just …

Announce it without giving away too much information,

then hang up. Make 'lodger' sound natural, like saying, I'm the lamp. Don't expose the formulation.

Are you OK?

Say, Sorry, I'm a minor yet neutral source of income, I'm a tin of tuna! Useful, undelicious. Sprung from nowhere with juice that doesn't amount to anything. Say, I'm sorry! Must go! Hang up.

There's no one here, you say.

But you're there.

Yeah. I'm here.

Moffa the post

As I was saying, it is because of Moffa's car that I don't like the idea of driving, assuming that every journey is a treacherous gamble with the weather, the traffic police and the engine itself. I feel sick at the opera, I can feel it as a miasma of petrol, the smell of wine gums and my car-sleep nightmares. Once we drove north for seven hours to sleep on someone's floor, missing school and a dentist appointment, just for her to understudy Irina from *The Seagull* for an actress who was nearly French and immediately went on to have a successful comeback in Hollywood. Moffa stepped in and out of the play while I sat writing hate lists in the dark at the back of the auditorium, ignored the dress rehearsals and opening nights, fell asleep in Moffa's lap if she was there, fed myself with instant soup and salted peanuts stolen from the green room where I was mildly teased by office staff. There was some attempted arrangement for me to go to school with some theatre member of staff's daughter who was two years younger and a hair-sucking fool. A boy in her class called me 'sexy' and the teacher patronised me for getting 8/10 in a maths test. After that I refused to go or hid so they couldn't make me. I didn't see Moffa much but there was a photo in the local paper of her and the actress leaving a restaurant one night holding hands.

The Hollywood actress and Moffa stayed friends for years after the play, initially writing to each other intensely, planning a trip to Los Angeles that Moffa would never make. The actress remained in our lives as a story at Moffa's parties and in very occasional post. We'd both run to the door at the sound of the post. Her memory of the actress was like an incense Moffa would occasionally burn to make herself come to life, it seemed to make up for a lot of material things that were missing, a superstitious stand-in. One Christmas morning we sat in bed with Lucozade and popcorn, ready to watch a film on the small television—a film that she turned out not to be in and that we slept through anyway.

You wiggle

Was it revenge on the grandmother or a way to regain something you needed anyway? Did you visit the professor in your bed vest? Did you slip down the stairs in the middle of the night like a spider, transmitted through the living room of comfy sofas? What a swerve. The tact of your messages was enough to be nothing, but was something: Awake? Yes. You? No. Ha. Shame. Now the boredom, the brace and the allure have to mix. Standardise your pose, enforce a libido. Wet your mouth at his door then push it open. He is standing by the door wearing a bathrobe and pulls you into the room. You kneel on the bed and let him start on you, but all he does is kiss you so you take over, pull clothes off and open your legs, aiming for the moment when it's already happened. How was it? Did you take out the good illusion and fold it away? Did you obliterate a fantasy? Fuck his brains out. Did it vary, did you wiggle?

Did you wear yourself out? You did, you did. How did the cradle of his shoulders block your view? Where did you look? You can get out of there now. Grab one of the nicer towels and shift backwards, lock onto fate then retreat to your own room. Every step back upstairs loads into your centre, aching your shapes, pummelling outwards. You're smiling. I'm smiling.

It would be terrible if when fleeing back to your bed, you found all of the upstairs doors open. It would be so strange for there to be no sign or sense of the mother and child, no sound or atmosphere, just late dark, minus life. Imagine the silence without them and the hollowness of the house. A child wakes from a nightmare and there's no one there. You imagine it without them. Get into bed and stare at the ceiling. (What did he say? Was it, Yes hit me! What did he call you, was it Slut! Minx? The choral strain! Bitch! Ripping!) Lie back and read one page of the text set for your course tomorrow. Roll over and turn off the lamp, try to sleep a little if you can. It's obvious.

In the morning the house is so empty and soundless you wake up early. You dress quietly and pack your bag without eating anything, not even muesli. Take a banana just in case. Where is the mother and her little girl? There is nowhere they could already be so early in the morning is there? But what do you know about it, about the workings of a domestic life? You hang in the air between the front door and the sofa absorbing the lesser feeling of a house in the morning that has only you in it. From behind a wall the professor coughs, you leave.

Moffa the shoe shop

Having to be impermanent but ready—like an imminent alarm clock, encountering street names and weather, sacrificing one plan and one direction in favour of another, regarding a nice tree, dead tree, common threat, bad design, couples walking together, sunrise, nature in reality against my idea of it—is a socially inherited condition. What I mean is: that same morning I woke up very early and went for a walk in a nearby woods. The trees were still warm from summer and the mud was hard, the temperature in general more like a room in a large museum than a woods. A man in blue waterproofs asked me if I had seen a little blond boy. He was worried but containing it, trying to sound amused. I said, I don't know. He said, What do you mean you don't know? I'm looking for my son. I said, That is my genuine answer, I don't know. I saw them together half an hour later in matching jackets climbing over a stile. The man flashed me an odd look: triumphant, ashamed, superior, stupid bobble hat and beard. That's all that happened, the birdsong was nice. Walking gives a blank day something to say for itself but it won't last, like everything, the feeling of action plateaus. While walking I decided I needed to find a way to be in Moffa's town that wasn't accidents and bumping into people. Before announcing myself to Moffa I needed a plan or something more like a ruse, for me and for her, a ruse for me to have come back to her without having come back for her.

With cold ears I returned to the flat to have tea and toast on the sofa. I ate half a pear and half a banana, then the other half of the pear and banana, drank some more tea and scratched where something had bitten me. What an empty life. I gazed at Kav's bedroom door. There was muck on my sleeve that wouldn't come off. I yawned and went to the window. A plane flew over Moffa's garden then away across the sky towards a border. Good for it. Its flight path drew out a vague awareness that she could be out there, walking in circles wearing a poncho. I wanted to go back out, to shop this time, to synchronise more. Choosing shoes from the two pairs lying in havoc on the mat took a moment; one pair had just been kicked off after a long walk; the others were loafers, uncomfortable though smarter, falling apart a little. At least it was a problem that gave me a reason to shop: I needed new shoes.

At the exit to my block of flats a woman with a confident voice was standing at the door saying goodbye to a man who was carrying two cans of paint to his car. She had said something very funny to him, some hilarious parting shot that made him shake the paint tins until he had to set them down and wipe his eyes from laughing. I snuck around the woman holding the door open with a meaningless Thank you and passed the car where the man was laughing. He let out one last moaning guffaw when he saw me then went quiet, stiffening in recognition. The woman must have recognised me too. She called out something vague like, Mind how you go, love. Moffa's people. Horrible. The main door clicked shut as the woman stepped out to mutter to her friend a word I didn't want to hear. They watched me go. The sole of one of my loafers finally came loose and started flapping as I walked away. Give me half a grandparent or a motorbike, please. Give me some small armour against this town. This pinhole camera. Niche secular quirks. Bonkers. Frightening. Fate-aggrieved people looking at me.

* * *

There was a stray cat in the shoe shop. It was hiding under children's pumps with serious eyes that caught mine as I felt the width of an ankle boot. We exchanged looks. Mine said, I don't know why I'm here either. I felt my toes moving in the boot, decided to buy them. While the shop assistant was getting the left boot and the box that I intended to refuse I got a better look at the cat and was struck by how much it looked like Gerri. Gerri the cat, I imagined her, after all these years. I trod a circle to test the heel on my right foot, leaving the other foot in the now more unbearable loafer. Gerri would be nearly thirty years old now. Time felt very far away from me, the difference between my feet in odd shoes.

Moffa had walked through the front door with Gerri as a surprise when she was in one of her softy months, declaring that it was my cat. Sadly Gerri left after a year or so for life with a better-resourced neighbour. She'd come back to see me sometimes when I was in the yard with a magazine and the sun was in the right place. I'd tickle her belly, shyly. I tried to tickle the stray cat's belly in the shoe shop but touched some scabby skin. The shop assistant ran it out of the shop hissing and saying something about it having fleas. I paid for the shoes and left. The door made a noise like a turkey. Outside, I imagined myself standing in the same high street as a much younger woman dodging *looks*. Odd looks, dirty looks, amused looks that came at me constantly, looks that said, O you're the daughter of *that* woman, who has *those* parties, how old are you now?

Wearing my new boots already, I carried the old loafers down the street, tucked under my arm like a portmanteau of hope and defeat. Suddenly it occurred to me that I'd bought them from that very same shoe shop. Silly me. After years of getting uglier and more comfortable the dirty old loafers have walked me right back here. I dropped them into a bin as soon as I could and as soon as I did the new boots started scraping the skin on my heels. After two minutes walking was agony. What else happened?

I saw Vicky. She was at the bus stop singing to herself and it was really her, a real being from the past still singing. She had a toddler-aged daughter who had a runny nose and was nearly as big as her. We hugged. She asked me where I was going and I said my feet hurt. Vicky used to act out entire scenes from sketch shows because she loved the voices. On the walk to school she'd recite twenty minutes of a man forcing his flatmate to eat rotten meat so he could masturbate to Miss World alone. Vicky wasn't too shy to contort her face into any grotesque shape to get the routine right. One sketch would last the whole way to the school gates. If there was time she might wander on all fours into the road and make the school-run traffic go round her. I'd laugh myself into a mess.

I told Vicky I lived in town now and she responded with a scandalised *Noooo*. The bus arrived and we both had to lift her screaming daughter on board. Vicky explained it was her first time on a bus since her grandad accidentally left her on the X80. Vicky's adult maternal voice sounded like a character from one of her routines. We talked about her dad who lived in a block of flats we passed, one without net curtains on the third floor. He was ten years younger than every other dad and once occupied a full month of my adolescent fancy. I would imagine he needed to walk me back to Moffa's through the park, and would grab my hand and lead me to a bench, undo my shirt and give me love bites and money. He was so handsome and funny. Now he's on the sofa staring at the floor about to miss another bin day—I imagined.

I told Vicky about my course, I said, it's like a sub-sub-subset of about eight different practices, very hands-on and very theoretical, then explained that it would take a while to sink in. Vicky said that she did her first-aider last week. Probably more useful, I said. Not a career though, Vicky said. What is?! I threw my arms up stupidly. We both knew a career is a way to get rid of yourself through equipment. It's how people anthropomorphise their basic financial needs. You have to want a career before you have permission to eat and have housing. I work in Sharon's Lettings once a week, Vicky said. We laughed.

On the walk to school Vicky used to wrap her flask of squash up in her PE towel and carry it like a newborn baby, stopping awkward men on their way to work and asking in a posh voice, What do you think? Shall we name him after you? Vicky looked at me like someone looks at an old friend who's fallen over and asked what I was doing for money. I liked that she asked me that. I told her that I'd got until the 28th next month to work that out, deciding not to say why there was enough in my account for me to sublet a room in a small flat and do little else every day except hurt my feet in town. People take time out. Isn't that so? People take time out of the time they had taken out and without meaning to, fold themselves into irreducible non-existences. Well Vicky, I might have explained, I was having one of those days in one of those phases in one of those lives. Vicky would have understood, she didn't expect things to be easy. She was smart and accepting.

But could I have stopped myself from talking? From telling her how there's no simple way to answer anything like that however simply she asked. I was speeding away from being young and motivated, where the question of what one is doing and whether one is doing something for, or in order to have, money is expected, but was now becoming a risky thing to ask. My non-answer and my answers could go on forever. Sweet, painful and peculiar. The backstory to every month's rent payment always is though isn't it? As a public drinking fountain trickles mundanity we dribbled to life, Vicky, no further questions. But she didn't push the point, she just spoke the words, What are you doing for money? I could've said *how*. At least it was easier to answer than the unasked Why? If she'd asked, Why, *why* are you here? I would have frozen. I don't know why!

The answer to How? was that all summer I had worked without being paid. Vicky might have said, What?! And I would have said, starting at a starting point, that after finishing my course and leaving the house where I lodged with a mum and her tricksy child, followed by a few panicked weeks of looking for any job or way to earn that followed the logic of my doing the course, I received an email sent to all alumni advertising for a research assistant for a Mass Mind Wandering Experiment. My friend Judy and I both applied and both got jobs. I got it! she'd written first, and all day I was depressed in a library checking my emails until closing time when I got the email too. MaMiWE was a group of social scientists and psychologists investigating the effects and processes of mind wandering, conducting a massive investigation into the meandering thoughts of the public by asking a large, but in my opinion not large enough, group of volunteers to wear a buzzer in their ear that went off at random times. The buzzer was meant to catch any wandering thought that wasn't 'relevant to the task or occupation the participant was engaged in.' They had to page me exactly what they were caught thinking or where their mind had wandered to, in no more than seventy characters. My full job title was Thought Scribe. I was sat at a desk, in a different building to Judy, every day over summer receiving pager messages from participants to type into a database: 'What if my shoe was another mouth?,' 'Make new treehouse to win prize and afford care-home,' 'I want nice teeth,' 'Sex with the bus driver right now,' 'My daughter is haunted,' 'How to make husband feel bad for saying that about Penny.' I added some tags; #FAMILY #MURDER #SEX #SUCCESS. The work was straightforward transcription and data entry but it genuinely *was* related to the course. I was a warden of sorts, for what people were thinking but not doing. I was allowed a break for a really disturbing one but never took it. None of them were that bad. Could I have a break for my own thoughts if they got bad? I had asked. The answer was no. Otherwise I enjoyed the work and the feeling that my course had led me into it, that it was paying off, was tying money to plans. Knowing it was a very short-term contract and, despite the office being in the basement of a busy research centre that smelt funny and made me smell funny, nowhere near Judy, was mostly forgivable. The hitch was no one could work out who had hired me, not officially. The project was funded and administered by at least six institutions and four different funding bodies so it took the entirety of my notional contract for there to be an actual contract and for me to be logged on to payroll. I received three months' pay in a lump sum on my very last day, having lived on near-nothing all summer; having walked for an hour to and from work every day; having stayed with my two-month-senior half-sister as a favour that I'll be forever emotionally punished for, and the less said about her the better; having eaten mostly humous and oatcakes; having stolen pound coins from my half-sister's bedroom to buy them; having run out of washing powder and used hers until she started hiding it, then stealing her knickers instead of washing my own, then getting used to stealing things from her and eventually helping myself to everything from shampoo to spirulina; having budgeted my outgoings into nothing, but having just sat, evening upon evening, still and tense, twitching between work hours, sweeping the stern grey flank of an oatcake through the same-coloured gunk until the plastic shone through and dumping it in my mouth.

To Vicky's amusement I told her I was subletting a flat in Mills Hump Gardens from some guy, no, I'd never met him. I told her my theory that he was in rehab. Alone? No idea. No, you. O. Yes, but only until the other flatmate appears. Do you know anyone called Kav? I asked. Her daughter's sobbing was too loud for us to talk any more. I smiled at her and she cried. This is me! I shouted as Moffa's house came into view with my stop a little before it. I rang the bell three or four times then wobbled down the stairs saying Goodbye, goodbye Vicky. That's when everything went weird.

The bus driver had already started letting people on so my exit was blocked. In the corner of my eye I noticed Madden was sitting on the lower deck just behind me. I rushed to get off the bus before he saw me. A man carrying a long tube was slowly paying his fare, I tried to push past him but a small boy ducked under the tube and ran upstairs, leaving his grandparents on the pavement shouting after him. Moving out of his way I kicked over a shopping bag full of plant pots next to the priority seat. The shopper squawked, I fell into the man with a tube, a dachshund started growling from the side. The grandparents and a young person using crutches were trying to board. I felt Madden becoming alert to me and watching me tumble around. No pub quiz, no pub quiz, I thought, becoming panicked. I finally stepped down from the bus, trying to avoid the grandparents—all in my painful new boots—and fell. With both knees pounded against the floor I remembered Vicky saying when we were young that she never wanted children.

After the sudden pain calmed I looked up and saw Moffa's front door a few yards from me. It was now painted green with a ginger-cat mural on the wall. I stared at it until I created a hallucination of the door opening, and Moffa stepping out wearing a long cardigan with fur trim and red beads, looking like a hawthorn tree, dragging a wheeled suitcase and a lamp. Imaginary Moffa walked straight past without acknowledging me at all except to say out loud and indirectly to the air, Up, up, up you get, before the whole world follows you. I watched her strut to the door of a waiting imaginary limousine and carried on watching as the chauffeur hoisted her bag into the boot. I watched still as the driver helped Moffa get into the back of the car, close her door then ferry her away somewhere. I brushed my knees and saw Vicky watching me from the window of the bus. She was laughing.

You repeat

Give me something else to think about. Have you gone back to the professor? Yes you have, you go regularly. Going to his room has become a habit. It is your new angle. All visitations find routines, so how does this one go? He doesn't get up any more, you feel your way to the bed in the dark, find him without speaking, be found, garments down, aside and up. He asks you about your day once he's already inside you. You don't reply or say anything. From what angle do you see his face? From the same angle a son would look up at you. At the end of rocking you on his lap he puffs, you push back like you've fallen under a raft, he lies heavy on you and puffs again. You lie still to reabsorb enough energy to leave. Somewhere in the seconds after the sequence there is another night to retreat to. It gives you shelter just before you feel stuck in the oven-hot heap. That's when there's a chance to divide; the three parts of the sum of you open, they divorce and glow, then settle.

Shall we reflect on this? You want something in exchange for these nights. You want some small gestures that repeat the scene on the TV screen and its feeling. On the mornings after you visit the professor's bed, while you're both in the kitchen but the mother is not up yet, you pick little fights with him to do with the girl's breakfast. That's too much for her, you say or, Those plates need to be done right now. He goes along with it, probably because he expects women to be 'bickery,' and squabbles back over what to read to her while she eats. That's not her book for this week! The girl accepts whatever obscure behaviour she encounters from adults and plays into it, siding with one of you. This, when she sides against you with the professor, is when you feel a kind of climax, the end of a triangle. You stormily do the washing-up and every so often turn to the side to tell the girl to hurry up. When the mother comes into the room, dynamic and ready in skin-tight jeans, saying, Morning everyone, and cuddles her daughter, you and the professor drop your acts. The professor checks his phone and leaves, smiling to everyone. Your landlady tells you to leave the washing-up and you sadly walk away from the kitchen.

One afternoon you take the game with the professor a little too far. On your way back to the house from college you decide to get off the bus early at the medium-sized Co-op and 'do a shop.' What is this? I can't really see or understand it, you can't afford 'a big shop' can you? And you're already eating into your overdraft, but you push the shopping trolley around the aisles pretending to be … stressed? Picking up bottles of bleach, boxes of cereal, fruit, toilet roll, biscuits, you fill two shopping bags which seems to give you the feeling you were after and come into the kitchen through the back door. As planned, the professor is there cooking his supper and the girl is running in and out of the room with a quiz she invented. Pigs or Cows X Bats or Monkeys X Are the fish dead? Y/N. You put the bags on the floor and ask the professor for help. He automatically obliges. As he puts things in the fridge the girl pulls chocolate from the grocery pile and asks if it's for her, To have now? Not before your tea, you say.

Your landlady comes into the room and is confused, she looks at the shopping like a small insult but leaves it alone, worn out from her day. She says something about taking the money out of your rent but she's not invested in what she's saying. She takes the girl away for her bath and the professor moves humbly to the living room to watch the news.

Moffa I can feel

I say the word 'just' a lot because I don't stop moving. If someone called me I'd just be a minute. If I pulled the big red curtains across the stage of my life and they fell on me I'd say, Pardon me, the curtains are just on my head.

* * *

As the tap dripped into the steel sink of my sour kitchenette that night I remembered a fantasy I used to have about getting engaged. Except that's not true, the fantasy was not about the act of being engaged, only about announcing it to Moffa. Anything about the fiancé or the actual wedding didn't feature at all. The peak of the fantasy was the moment I said to Moffa, who would be sitting in her armchair facing the TV sucking a slice of pineapple, Guess what, I'm getting married. In the fantasy Moffa would turn to look at me with bright delighted eyes, clap her hands and screech, then sing, then call her friends. She'd throw an engagement party in her tiny house, it would be cramped full of her lipsticked people with swinging jewellery and paisley scarfs, there'd be boxes of wine on the table and dozens of small bowls full of olives and pretzels. The party was where my fantasy often got complicated, straying in multiple directions. Sometimes I'd dance with Moffa and people would Cheers! us with their drinks, or in the more realistic versions I'd be mostly ignored and then go to sit in the small bedroom full of Grandma's things, feeling awkward and overwhelmed. The fiancé, whoever it was, some puff of smoke in a V-neck jumper and shirt, would limply knock on the door to see if I was OK. I'd stubbornly say, Fine, then I'd hear him go to the toilet because the boxed wine disagreed with him. I'd sit on the tiny bed and realise I'd embarked on a serious relationship with this constitutionally weak man just to have something to say to Moffa. I was doing it again now, I was back in the daydream picturing myself being warmly congratulated after I'd delivered the shock news, the huge piece of information, That's why I'm back! The moment of declaring, that's all I wanted, to feel life reflecting off someone's delighted face onto mine. Clap, sing, call some friends.

Or Moffa would just say, Eugh God, why?, then carry on watching TV and I'd be left sitting still, not speaking, looking at my fingernails in the worst century ever.

You wear a towel

The morning sun feels too ready, the day is thickening ahead of time. It's late. You've woken up in the professor's bed. As you realise this you feel your bowels pinch. The room reeks with strangeness. You don't want to turn and see Professor Dommer, not in daylight, not his squished emerging face with red marks on his nose. Grab your little bundle of clothes and run upstairs, quickly. But it's too late, the girl is awake and thumping around looking for you. Shakily dash from his bedroom into the downstairs shower room and wet yourself then wrap a found towel around without drying, thinking, the wetter the better.

That's not your towel. The girl discovers you dripping wet, standing in the middle of the living room. As you begin to say, Yes, I'm here, I had a shower but then I got *really* thirsty so had to come out to drink *six* glasses of milk before I could get dressed. The mother's footsteps follow and she arrives behind her daughter to regard you and your sodden hair. All right? She had to drink some milk, says the child, six glasses! The girl marches into the kitchen with the rallying cry, Six glasses, I want six glasses of milk. Sixty glasses. I want a kitten! The dog comes to sniff you. The wrong towel is also a giveaway. You try to look hapless and lovable as you glance at the mother then sidle past her, up to your open-doored bedroom to dress.

Professor Dommer is in the kitchen with them when you come down, talking loudly to the girl, holding his whole slice of margarined toast in one hand. The mother is laughing along with whatever prank he is teasing the girl with, something about good swimmers growing gills. You steer clear of both of them to get a bowl from the cupboard, pour some muesli, the mother passes you the milk, then some tea which is warm and ready for you, but she doesn't look at you. You feel sick, it'll be a hard day today on the course. You'd like to go to bed and tell them you're ill, but that's not an option for you. Your bedroom is needed. You'll be in the way.

Moffa the bathroom

Nobody warns girls that periods come with terrible diarrhoea. As if to make your body elementally profound but urgently stupid, full of whisking rats, low beating tailbone pain erasing nice new adult human ideas. As she clings to herself the bathroom becomes a place a girl collapses into, a retreat to spend deep time fixating on an unfurling strip of rubber grouting or a drip of candle wax, plotting the self, resting eyeballs while evacuating rushes of godonlyknows. And so, a girl learns to associate the bathroom with physical and spiritual revision. A triangular place where there is safety and reflection. Scales, but no point of reference. A mirror, but also a homely light. The only room with a lock and a source of water, that's the room for me, she thinks. Leave all the myths of womanhood outside and contemplate, deeply calibrate. Without fuss, the girl that I was would disappear into the bathroom for an afternoon, hours of time, doing hardly anything except assessing and learning the possibilities of privacy. Understanding exactly how I looked, how I felt, how I could do press-ups, how far hairbrush handles fit inside me, how fast I could plait one side of my hair, how I could laugh with my mouth open or closed, whether I could sing. The pleasure of living somewhere ever since was contingent on the bathroom and whether I felt the solace of the acoustics and light.

The bathroom in my new sublet was just large enough to decamp in. It was 'recently renovated,' inhumanely white and lit, but a bath's a bath. Or so I thought. I couldn't seem to run my thirty-four gallons of scorching water and slowly dial myself into it without hearing Kav's key, or thinking I heard it, twisting in the front door. I heard it then I got out and locked the bathroom door. The water would not feel this good again. I heard the key. I got up and looked outside the door, saw nothing but a very small empty flat, returned to the diminishing triumph of heat. The threat of Kav lay on the surface like another steam.

My wet arm in the bathwater looked like something. I did not like it. My legs looked alien. I wiggled them. My stomach shone then blurred. I blurred. Was I returning to my teenage self? Was I a hip then a bone in a stew? What to contemplate? Chin on knees. Being a teenager, being in the bathroom in Moffa's house. I remembered walking into the bathroom and seeing something. It was my headache. I saw what I wanted. What I saw? A field of porpoise skin. A close up of roses after rain. Why did I walk in? I was just that age when I had needed to release my happening belly and had crept up the stairs too lightly, had gone into myself too early. I hadn't listened out or been careful. I saw. In the bath, a division of silks and furs. A triangulation of wolf noses and seaweed. A duo of bathers. Two women with a rich clutch of care between them. They were laughing. She was washing her hair. Moffa and Pearl in the bath. A two-headed bird. Moffa was lying back against our young lodger, both of them facing the taps and away from me, where I haunted the door for a second, just a second, then curled away. But I saw Pearl's and Moffa's legs bridging the water, ladder and glistening. Pearl poured a cup of water over Moffa's head and stroked her hair back. Moffa absorbed the bliss. I didn't know what to do. I was shocked, by the care and the water, the attention between them. I wanted it. The hot do.

I heard Kav's key again.

You kick a bike

In the suburbs the evening birds honk and yip as you walk around the cul-de-sac towards your landlady's house, past the boat that never goes to sea, past the taxi which will be gone soon for the night. Before you can get your keys in the door the mother lets you in. All right? she says in a light sing-song voice. She's wearing her cleaning clothes but her make-up is perfect. Your hair and skin are fried from the air in the classroom and bus. Thank you, you say, yes, how are you? She watches you take your coat off and then asks if the landline rang when she was out yesterday. You say, Oooh I don't know. She watches you drag off your shoes. Your landlady wants to be frank with you about something. She says, I'm sorry for what's happening. Your puzzled face is hopeless. O? You think she means the professor, that she'll ask you to leave. She apologises for the little girl's 'acting up.' You pick up your bag of soup and bread to take to the kitchen. She says the girl is processing a lot of difficult things at the moment. You agree, but you're not sure what with. Then the little girl calls your name from the garden and you smile at the mother before obediently going to see her daughter out on the dark patio.

The child has found a dead bird and, for reasons too encrypted in childhood for anyone to understand, wants to show it to you. She leads you to the bottom of the garden whispering things like, You won't believe this. When you get all the way to the dampish shed, where the lights from the kitchen can't quite reach, true enough there is a grey plump corpse dropped centrally on a square of concrete. The girl squats down, scowls at the dead pigeon then up at you. Don't tell Mummy. Don't touch it. I won't, Mummy doesn't like it when birds are dead. It so happens she has a plastic star-mounted wand in her hand and uses it to whack the ground repeatedly near the bird. You are a little lost about what to do with her. You take her hand and lift her to standing. In retaliation she hits your buttocks with the wand. Don't do that. I didn't touch the bird. That's not why. Piss. Don't say that. I hate ... Joe at the back!

After hitting you again she hugs you and leans her minor weight against you. You imagine what you look like from above: girl, dead bird, lodger. Strange archetypes. The mood changes again with the sound of her mother's voice from the kitchen announcing her meal of meatballs and pasta tubes. The girl's sudden flight has all the violence you are used to now. What does hurt is snagging your ankle on the pink bike lying abandoned on the lawn as you chase after her. Your shin will be bruised for five days. Back inside the girl is weeping into her mother's arms, upset about the dead pigeon, its horrible bloated body. In attempting to make it clear that you did not lead the child outside to view it against her will, you overly criminalise her, saying, I don't know why she wanted to look at it. I don't know why she likes dead things so much. Bringing up this private information that was told to you in adult confidence greatly offends the girl. She screams into her mother's chest. You attempt to make a joke, then stroke her back, but she flinches from you and cries some more. The mother nods quietly with her eyes closed, indicating that she knows, she knows, letting you off the hook and dismissing you at the same time. You retreat to your bedroom in feeble, slow steps, then climb under the duvet, pulling your bag up to your chest to retrieve half a sandwich that you eat in bed while scratching your shin and watching a house renovation programme on your laptop.

Maybe tonight you will message the professor and make a plan for your usual time of half past midnight. It will be the first time since you were nearly caught. Will you be less quiet and less careful? Perhaps you just don't care any more. Order him to do something new? Maybe you stay and talk to him about his day and let him stroke your back. Stare at the patterns on the bed clothes. Maybe he assumes an intimate eye contact and says that you're in a funny mood tonight, and you become secretly furious at his claim to know your moods. Outrageous. Frightening. Familiarity from habit is hard to avoid. Or will you be much more quiet and much more careful? To the point where you hardly breathe or move. It has to be one of these. No, I don't know, it should be obvious. Maybe, and this feels like the most likely, you will set an alarm on your phone then sleep right through it. But that's OK. Feeling the absence of your body from where it was promised is still thrilling. The moment passes in miniature sublime. Think about it.

Moffa an email

Today I emailed my subletter about Kav: Hello! Will Kav come? I wrote. Am I likely to meet this Kav anytime soon? I wrote. Just wondering if Kav was going to arrive, do you happen to know at all? I hope you're well and it's going OK. The flat is lovely. I'd love to stay on if that's OK? You said a few months or maybe a year? Let me know, I wrote.

You flyer

What are you doing this weekend as the autumn sets in proper? I imagine you handing out flyers back in the city. You are wearing a fleecy pullover that's a little too big, absorbing light rain and vape smoke outside a crowded arts venue. Groups of people sit on benches in clumps practising being attractive. A man takes a flyer from you without looking away from his phone, a woman drinking from a can also takes a flyer and folds it away, a teenager sitting with their parents looks intently at their feet until you move on. You have so many flyers still. A made-up song the girl was singing on the toilet that week is stuck in your head, *stick your eyes in the world and have babies. Stick your eyes on your boobies and have friends.* Just put them on the tables, Ann Yosy says, and then we can go. She's angry with you. The flyers are for an activist art event she has organised and will be modelling upcycled fashion in. You are helping her distribute flyers because you're staying at hers tonight. You try to help out with one of her many enterprises every time you stay at hers for the weekend instead of payment. Ann Yosy always asks about the professor, the mother, the little girl, but you've never mentioned Ann Yosy to anyone in the house. This must be because no one in it has ever asked you about your life outside the house apart from your immediate day.

This friend of yours is very strong. The inner-city house she brokered with the landlord's agent is strong too, but chaotic and noisy. There is no way to occupy it shyly and it doesn't really suit you but Ann Yosy persists. Whenever she feels you being awkward she grabs you by the waist, carries you to the stairwell and puts you on the stairs. That is how she manages your friendship and your reliance on her. She wrestles you, you giggle, you are like a mother and child, like boyfriend and girlfriend, like two monkeys. If you are on the sofa she will pretend not to see you and sit on your lap then ask where you are. Sometimes Ann Yosy comes into the kitchen and picks you up then continues the conversation with the other housemates, holding you in the air. You keep a straight face hanging inches away from the floor. Ann Yosy has made a special space on the bookshelf for any post that arrives for you and washes your forgotten knickers and socks. She could manage your life on top of hers as easily as opening a tin can. When you are clumsy, when you put things in the wrong place, she teases you just the right amount. You play into her teasing, finding tenderness in her charge. The other two housemates,

Tully and Asher, are so close it's heartbreaking. Tully has a photo of Asher naked on their wall, Because it's *gorgeous*. They're both skinny, like deer, and run upstairs with boots on. They appear together in response to either of their names. Their bedrooms are across from each other at the top of the house so their noises travel the full height of the building. Up and down they race and sing. Ann Yosy navigates them like elements. The housemates treat you as part of the household without question, your stories about the little girl delight them. They put their heads together and ask to hear what she's said this week and coo over your bruises from her kicks. Funny things the girl had said have become household catchphrases; if one housemate is offering the other a beer from the fridge they might say, I love a lot my drink, or if one of them is in the bathroom the other housemate will knock on the door and shout, This kid needs to dump before it's my birthday party. You love the bathroom. It is rotten and mouldy but Ann Yosy has adorned it with the integrity of someone committed to a different life, its beauty and solace. A bather can lie back and feel at ease among spider plants and candles. One mismatching towel per person, a tattered bathmat, the filthy grouting and the '90s tiles underneath, a large window next to a bus route and street lamp. There is a box room going for £500pm, plus bills.

Ann Yosy orders you both flutes of gassy beer and a bowl of chips then tries to get to the bottom of things. So who is this guy? she asks. What guy? The one you live with. I don't live with anyone. I thought you lived with an old man who you have sex with but find annoying and he's in his fifties so sometimes he isn't that hard but you can't mention it and have to do it anyway? How does that work? O we don't live together, you say, we just live in the same house. Most of the time. He's nice. Ann Yosy tuts and puts her phone down saying, Losers, to whoever was on her phone. She looks up and says, I love you. But I don't get you. Why don't you just date someone? There are loads of nice people around. You laugh and that's an appropriate response. Life is an easy, playful dialogue when it isn't yours to do. Ann says, Come on! You laugh again. I mean, fine, do it once or twice for fun and then stop, but how long has it been? You realise and tell her that it's been nearly eight times. Gross, she says. And the landlady doesn't know? You come back from college, play with her little girl and then go downstairs and have sex with this old man? We're old, you say, the world is dying. Everyone is old, except the twenty-year-olds you pick up. Show me a picture, she says. I don't have one. Tell me his name. You say his name before taking a large, nervous swig of beer. Ann Yosy looks him up on her phone, stares blankly at the screen for a moment then convulses, nearly bursting her mouth of beer. What the ... what is allure-memory-tracking? Why is he blindfolding that woman? Stop, you say, he's a scientist. He looks like Hugh Bonneville. I hate you. O dear o dear, Ann Yosy says, what are we going to do with you. This course finishes in the spring, the body-slapping training. Am I right? TriTouch Therapy. And yes, you say. Then you'll come and live with me, says Ann Yosy, move in properly? We're sorting out the garden, Moose is building a summer house. We'll sort you out. You take a chip and say crossly, Sort me out.

Moffa the course

There are nearly ten years between us in age but we are both thirty-something, the decade of a woman's life when her silhouette surfaces. The decade when self-mockery becomes genuinely hilarious while aloneness and the rotation of housing become more bathetic than tragic. I'm on my way out with not much intact except circumstance. We'll always have that.

Some things about this last month I don't understand. There was a stray cat in the shoe shop. Moffa is not here. I live with Kav. Kav's not here yet. You? You roll around. You pace through the house when you're alone, touching drawers, looking in mirrors. You steal some lacy knickers from the radiator. You look for a long time in the drawer you put the rent in. You tell the little girl you love her. I look in mirrors. I see thick, frizzy hair and my half-sister's frown. You see your father's chin and side wave of thin, dark hair. I yawn and let my eyes cloud. You yawn and pout your mouth.

We did the same TriTouch course. I understand that. You are doing the course that I did and that means something. I haven't thought about what got me onto the course for a while but it's good to remember the early stages of plans, ones I shared with other people. What is it that brings strangers of different ages and lives together to enrol on the same course at the same place, at the same time? Because we have too much money or not enough? It might be the promise of the syllabus and skill set; the want to know. It could be something as arbitrary as the hours of the day that you have to be there for class. Something as fluked as a timetable could attract a bunch of characters with similar access to loans and a shared optimism, despite the invariable turn of events they've lived so far. It is much of a muchness. Some people scroll down a brochure looking for something—anything—that might advance them, starting in the next month; other people have been working towards it for years, ticking off life goals. I just did it. The advert for the course suggested you could make a living turning your worst memories into healing techniques, 'powerful transformational tools' to improve lives, including your own! *Have the best year of your life*. I thought, that's the ticket. I turned up every day, except on a roving study day, with a pen and bottle of water, ready to return to learning and sit next to my friend Judy. The classroom remained bright when it was grey and wet outside. It was left smelling of the younger people from the hour before, with tables out of shape and empty energy drink cans. Me and my classmates would arrive and re-cohere the tables, saying Hi, catching tired looks and smiling, blinking away chlorine and screen time. At the front of the classroom there was space for demonstrations on a complex of plastic models, a screen for video clips which might be followed by some role play, or breakouts, or live participant volunteers, silent contemplation, group recitals of the core tenets, blessings from a special guest speaker. The tutor would arrive walking backwards into the room and carrying props. Into the ambience of stirred admiration the tutor would smile at everyone over her glasses, drop a tea bag into the small bin and start the class.

Everyone there was dedicated to the concept of earning while helping people, eventually. Dedicated to having a trade and an education, to the limits of a tradition and its brand-new trademark-registered method, its techniques and our flairs, to becoming part of an industry of practices, the story of its pioneers and renegades, the history of its theories and the interpretation of its theories, to embodying the theory with our hands and tools, to living out diagrams. What some had conceptualised, we would do; what we would do, others would conceptualise. We turned up to the 1960s site of ancient ideas with new instruments; a library of texts; a school of colleagues and peers; a certain number of hours to make sense of it; to align ourselves to a school of attitudes, then get to work. Don't appropriate, learn; don't rely on the state, become through learning what's therapeutic, become the means to ease the general public's ambiguous symptoms whether they can express what's wrong or not. Keep everything suspended and try to serve people who are in genuine need, as well as people who are *so* middle class and so heterosexual they're horrible; keep them going, we might as well. Half the group would give it a year trying to make it, the other half would do another course immediately afterwards. After all, a course is simply a lament. We do it to keep everything suspended.

You move

For the first time I wonder where you lived before this year. I know it wasn't straightforward, I know it was another complicated transaction. You've been rotating them all your life.

For a while your main address was an attic flat you had all to yourself in a hilly area on the outskirts of the city. Living there came about in the strangest way. Helping Ann Yosy hand out flyers again, this time for a comedy show, you stopped at a pub, and on one of the garden tables you met a sharply dressed woman with big sleeves who wanted to know more about the show. You had to invent some information, It's a hit. You'll never be the same again. She told you that you reminded her of her friend's daughter, so much so she was convinced that you were her friend's daughter. The woman's name was Beverly. You found that out when you bumped into her again in the toilets during the interval of the comedy show you had been flyering for a week later. It was terrible, that show, it was so bad! She joke-slapped your arm. You chatted and washed your hands. Beverly acted like she knew you very well. In the conversation with wet hands she asked where you lived and you said you were looking for somewhere, quite urgently in fact. Well then this is fate, she said. Beverly had a flat in this very borough that she only used when she had to be in town for work, you could rent it for a small amount if you were happy to leave occasionally and erase all evidence of yourself when Beverly needed to stay there for work. That was the last time you saw Beverly. The only communication you had with her from then on was by email or notes left on the stairs.

The flat was the less-nice top half of a large Georgian house opposite a hilly park. The keys were kept safe by a Scottish woman called Ava who wore Nike Airs and many bead necklaces, and who lived in the ground-floor flat and had done for twenty years. Through a separate front door to the side and up some stairs you found your flat. It had four small windowed rooms but only one room was comprehensive in any way; it was carpeted, and had a double bed and curtains. You were not allowed to use this room and had to keep the door closed at all times. The other three rooms, including the kitchen and bathroom, were full of storage boxes. There was no furniture or fridge, just an oven that was full of Beverly's pans, and in the tiny room at the back, no bed but instead five or six tightly tied bin bags full of her clothes. This was where you decided you should sleep so one of your first jobs was to find or construct a mattress. The need to do this didn't annoy you like it ought to have done. In fact you wandered across the small landing feeling grateful and lucky, confusing your life with the Scottish woman's downstairs.

On your first Saturday, with much physical effort you pushed most of the storage boxes in the kitchen into one mass, then lifted three of the smaller ones onto that gathering to create a sofa-shaped pile to sit on. You ripped open a bin bag, then another and then another until you found some sheets and a few cushions to put on the pile of boxes so it looked and even felt like a sofa. In one of the boxes was an old Freeview TV. You got it out and plugged it in, found a channel and sat down to watch something. All there was to watch was a programme about people self-building massive houses. It was hard to get comfortable on the boxes but you found a way. The structure was awkwardly high so you had to climb up, but you reassured yourself it was fine. Your legs swung as you watched multiple episodes of the self-build programme, sometimes getting emotionally invested, at other times watching with the same blank fascination with which you watched documentaries about the sea. When you jumped down from your self-build sofa the boxes shook. In a smaller storage box in the kitchen there was a toaster and a kettle. You would get used to eating one-tin meals or muesli with water. You learned to drink your tea black and eat what you bought that day. You would do furious star jumps every time the kettle boiled and for the full duration of its bubbling. It was a daily exercise.

On hot nights you lay on the bin bags in the small room with a magazine, listening to the Scottish woman in the garden flat below clinking plates and offering more fish to her guests. You could hear children refusing the fish and parent voices calling them back to the table. Some laughter. Some posh English accents saying, O Mother, please. You could hear grand oak chairs being scraped along the floor, piano music sometimes, and at other times you could smell bread. You wondered if Ava could hear you star-jumping. On a particularly muggy Saturday with no fridge and no plans the only thing to do was walk to the nearest supermarket to buy a bag of frozen peas and eat them like crisps as you sat on the boxes, listening to post arrive for Ava.

There is something satisfying about quaint survival but it runs thin. You tried to make the most of living alone. Having been encouraged to go on a date you allowed Ann Yosy to set you up with a man who sang in the choir she mastered. He messaged you every day in the week leading up to the date to find out if you liked pizza, if you liked walking, if you liked parks. He may have been good-looking in bad clothes, or bad-looking in good clothes, you weren't sure. It wasn't easy. But he wasn't dreadful. You brought him back to the flat, shared a dull conversation then useless sex. You straddled him to make sure it was over quickly. As he came your knee split open one of Beverly's bin bags and some beige chinos burst out. Afterwards you sat naked together on the boxes watching the self-build programme. In the middle of watching people concrete an enormous kitchen floor you did the worst-smelling fart of your life.

He pinched your waist and called you his little gasbag. You ignored him and scowled into the TV.

One Sunday you tried on all of Beverly's clothes. None of them were worth stealing, they made you look like the daughter of a corrupt politician. Every so often you would get an email from Beverly announcing her arrival the next day so you would spend the night cleaning and packing away your things, dismantling the sofa and repacking, putting the boxes back the way they were. You'd attempt to eat everything left over, which was usually a carton of yogurt kept in a bowl of water. You'd spray every room except Beverly's room with air freshener, sweep the floors, scrub the bathroom, and first thing in the morning, put the sheets you found to sleep on back into bags and into a wardrobe, then go to Ann Yosy's. One day you came back to the flat to find a friendly note from 'Bev' saying she needed more money and planned on letting the flat through Airbnb, Take care, Love Bev.

Moffa the Beehive

I woke up at 2 a.m. in Lee Martin's house after winning a round of the pub quiz and losing control. I understood all the steps I took to get there and accepted them along with consciousness. At 7 p.m. that evening I walked into the Beehive intending to play the quiz alone. Madden was doing a bit on the too-loud microphone about the price of petrol and while he was still speaking ushered me over to a table of people. Lee Martin was one of them, and I recognised one or two of his friends, some older, some younger. Just locals. In the corner I saw a table with Lloyd and his wife and another couple. Lloyd's wife had long, straight silver hair, she was beautiful, drunk already, and kept stabbing her husband with the shared pen. He laughed and cried, Murder! Domestic violence! Madden hung around their table flirting with Lloyd's wife. I suspected they were in a relationship. I briefly allowed myself to imagine Madden naked but turned away from the image like when I see sick in the street. Another table of drinkers vaguely pointed at me and waved. I threw myself into conversation with my team.

In the few hours I remember I drank a possible four pints of strong but fruity lager, finding the quiz surprisingly engaging and the group of friendly people with hooting laughs keen to welcome me. In between quiz rounds we talked about our work and everyone took a genuine interest in my course and techniques. I'd said, My personal massage is the shape of a bird with two heads. They smiled over their glasses and understood, or seemed to care. Their drunk faces were nice; strong angles and brows, eye bags that added a woeful kindness. I wrote the words 'drunken tart' down someone's spine. Does that feel nice? Yeah, it really does. I squeezed someone's waist and very slowly, indiscernibly whispered, *We want you out of here* into their neck. They leaned back, sinking into me in full relaxation and we hugged. Lee Martin let me tap his fingertips while I hummed a mantra. I felt special and accepted. That's all anyone wants. There was no reason not to get carried away and no shame in wanting to win. After some applause and shoulder pats due to my movie knowledge I was excited, I felt like Moffa, even quoted her and got laughs in recognition. Everyone knew her but that didn't feel like a punishment. Until an older guy said, O I remember her parties. Legendary nights, he boasted.

I didn't like that, I didn't want to hear it and prepared to go the toilets to hide for a bit. People shifted to let me pass and swallowed more beer. One night, he continued while I tried to squeeze out of the table, one night she disappeared upstairs then came back down dressed as a … I didn't hear. He slapped his leg in laughter … and then … in the street! I finally got free and stayed away for ten minutes. When I came back from the ladies there was a rum and Coke waiting for me and a picture round. I bashed my hand on the table and said, Come on! I recognised all the movie stars despite their distorted, collaged faces. We won a bonus round of drinks. I left with Lee Martin. We grabbed each other's arms and walked through the park. When I woke at 2 a.m. his bedroom span. I fell back to sleep in a funny position.

Lee Martin's house was a newly built, family-focused property. His long-term girlfriend was away. The atmosphere was cold. They really need some rugs and more pictures, I thought, Where's the care? How simple the rules are. We all live somewhere with a locked door. Is that true? We all live somewhere that represents our mother's smell. No … wait. We all eat where the table understands us … That's not it. To live is to know the softest version of what we can afford … and to want shelving, framed posters, and to always be a curious child, to have a beautiful child, to be always clashing with the music of leaving.

In the early morning, before the sun was really up and I could really speak in normal sentences, we drank coffee in his back garden and let the dogs play fight. After a digestive biscuit and some ibuprofen I left Lee Martin's house. I spent the rest of the day half-sleeping and clammy, crushed by a headache.

You drift

What about you? Your head is swaying then lurching, your body folded around a screen showing a baking competition finale. You are drifting off to sleep with your jeans still on and under the duvet. It's nearly the end of October. I watch your year pan out from here like paint spilling. At Christmas you will prepare to leave for two weeks. Before you go you will hand out gifts to the landlady and her daughter, small things you bought from the shop near your college: a dried-flower arrangement, sparkling wine, toy reindeer antlers for the dog. A colouring-in book for the girl. The landlady will give you some hand cream. When you return to your family at the address they've lived at for twenty-five years there will be new brothers- and sisters-in-law so you will sleep on the sofa to be woken every morning by two elderly cats roughly licking your scalp. There you will discover you are very tired and sleep most days, surrounded by plates of meat and nuts. Your father gives everyone money and your mother asks about everyone's health. You try to rub your mother's back, using a new technique, but a memory of being lost on the beach isn't working and you hurt her neck. The professor will message you most evenings in the lead-up to Christmas when he's had too much port. He'll say, Hey, and you'll reply, I'm sleeping on a sofa, he'll be concerned and use it as an excuse to refer to his bed in the house you both lodge in, then you'll say, I hate Christmas, and he'll reply, I think I miss you. You'll say, I hope you're having a nice time.

When you get back after New Year you will barely speak to him. Throughout January your time in the house with the mother, the child and the professor will alter. You will be tired and less able to concentrate on your course. The girl will seem suddenly older and apart from the hug she gives you when you return, pays you less attention. The mother will be distant and busy.

But back in this house you roll over in bed and your phone buzzes. It's still October, you have dozed off, you're there, and that little shake in your belly is me finding you. Erroneous lives passing.

Moffa a slightly bigger town

I lay on the floor of the sublet making a bird shape with my arms and legs. Kav could have walked in at any second. If he did I'd have had to say, Hi, just doing my exercises. What was I doing apart from movements? I was desperate to sleep. With Moffa still gone for who knows how long, my stay in the town where she lived was getting strange, dangerous and bulging in absurdity. I was bashing into things. Money was running out. There wasn't that much to begin with. Half as much as I thought I'd earned all summer. Today, I decided, was the day I ought to go looking for a job. A small, easy job. Something to pay for everything without breaking me. A sweet, people-focused company to look after me before I settled and the course settled in me and I moved on to being sorted. Wanting routines and employment I bandaged my heels, put an apple in my bag, and went on a trip to the nearest bigger town. The nearest bigger town was about fifteen minutes on the train from this one and was a place with more developed shops—for example, a library, nicer cafés, a town hall where teenagers skateboarded outside. I could go and come back with a fresh perspective.

That's not how it worked out. The day was scrappy and disjointed. I recommended myself for a job in a health and well-being shop which I then panicked about getting, to the point where I turned around and walked for half an hour back to the shop to withdraw my application on account of possibly needing to care for someone who would soon be very ill and need me every day. When I got back to the shop I grew indecisive again, remembering the reassurance of simply having a job. A job in a health and well-being shop would mean I could forge a narrative every day, a narrative that began with enrolling on a course and ended with practising the art of health. I could recount it every time the alarm woke me up at 6.30 a.m. and during all the things I'd have to do in order to get myself back to the shop where it smelled of cedar oil and liquorice.

The shop was hot and I dithered. I invented an excuse for my abrupt return: that I'd remembered I needed sleep. A different woman to the one I'd talked to before, a woman with a lot of blusher wearing a white laboratory coat, who drew out all the oooh sounds in her speaking, came out from behind the till and talked me through a number of expensive tinctures. With this one you pat, pat, pat, she demonstrated patting her face and neck, I've had real success, then added, It's oceany. I agreed. But I'm not looking for something to stop me looking tired, I want to sleep better. She nodded. Tell me more about what happens when you become awake during the night, does your heart race? Can you breathe? Sweat? How much sweat? I said so much I have to change my T-shirt and rotate the sheet. I'm sweating a lot lately. She looked serious, And thought patterns? Do you get stuck in repeating thought patterns? Sometimes, I said. (Neighbours' faces, Pearl in the bath, my landlady, your landlady, the girl, my cramping tummy, my triangle, your triangle.)

We selected some aromatherapy together, smells that halted thought cycles, and for a moment I really believed getting help for my sleeplessness was why I had gone back there and everything she said felt important. She wrapped the bottle of sleep remedy up carefully in gift paper and stuck a floral sticker over the fold. She then tied some decorative ribbon around the bottle and placed it in a small cardboard bag, handing it to me by its string handles which she had joined with a silver sticker. The second I held the bag my heart dropped at how much money I'd spent. Nothing halts thought cycles, nothing that you can spray on your pillow or drop on your tongue and I knew it. I took myself away from the bigger high street, via a charity shop to buy some vintage cups that might be nicer for my tea than the ones that came with the flat, and onto the train to stop me spending any more money.

On the walk across the car park of my station towards the sublet flat, I swung the little shopping bag by its handle, humming a casual tune. Life felt normal, it felt recurring and safe for a moment. I stopped, gulped. This bag. I had a bag. I had a bag before this. The feeling of this bag replaced the bag I should feel. My bag. The bag on the seat, still on the train. I tried to convince myself not to mind, to not know what a bag is. What is a bag? Keep walking. There was no other bag I needed except this one. But its contents. What was it I needed? Phone, wallet, keys. To go to my flat. Cannot get in. To call someone for help. Cannot. To buy something that might help. Cannot. All I was was in the car park. A van beeped for me to move. I did not have the bag I needed.

I went to my block of flats on the off chance but couldn't get past the main door at the bottom. I waited to tailgate a teenager but none came, I rang the bell of a few random numbers, waited there for a long time. Eventually a teenage boy did run out with a football. I didn't recognise him but he let me through and said, You're welcome, politely without eye contact. I walked up to the front door of my flat and breathed at it. It did not register to me as homely or openable. I knocked, paused, nothing, no one. I stared up and down the empty corridor of still front doors, and after a while went back outside to think.

You wave

Her daddy does arrive. I can and can't see this. He finally lets himself in. I can and can't see this. On a chilly dusk you return to the house at the usual time and find him on the armchair with the little girl collapsed on his lap as if she had fallen from the ceiling into his arms. Her face is creased from sleeping and one of her school shoes is dangling off her foot. You can hear her mother moving around upstairs shouting on the phone. He says Hello to you in a slow voice that reaches in and opens up a nerve in your head, that fills you like hot tea. You smile and put your bags down, he nods. The little girl waves to you. Waving back, you sit down, stand back up, you are not sure, I am not sure. He doesn't ask you any questions, he just sits still and holds his daughter, smiles at you without any fear of silence. I can see him now, there is an equal amount of peace and menace about him, there are occupations that would suit him, like a locksmith or gravedigger. Something caring and aggressive at once.

For two weeks he'll sleep on the sofa in the living room. Your landlady will hardly mention it or explain except to repeatedly say, I'm sorry about this. It won't be for very long, she'll say, I'm so sorry about this. The house is often empty when you come back from college and feels different, too empty to linger in. To begin with you just hide yourself in your room listening out for the door until late. In the mornings you look around the house. He is only there at night, mostly arriving when it's too late for you to go downstairs. As your thoughts dance in bed you consider yourself lying directly above him, the things you can and can't do, the things you are and are not, start to rotate. You have stopped going to the professor's bedroom. You have stopped doing a lot of things. They don't make sense. All you do is listen out for him in the movements of the house. Once you change and stop hiding, you start trying to be in the right room at the right time, ready to look, ready to soften, ready to be seen and teased and flirted with by the handsome father, who's good bad but not evil, his thick, wavy hair. Some things are still clear, the house still moves, all strangenesses are overridden by chores and routines. The washing-machine door is opened and closed, the landlady smiles, says, All right? The tension is as conspicuous as the washing machine's banging but all anyone can do is shower, drink tea or coffee then leave.

In between leaving and staying there are freshly creeping moments of excitement in the house. Something about the game you had with the professor has another stage. Much more real, much more dangerous, much more like it, isn't that right? It dawns on you that your fling with the professor was the rehearsal for a new idea that's forming. You know how to move, how to act, what to pick up and how to stand, how to show that you're ready and willing to play. One night you creep all the way to the kitchen to present yourself in nightwear when you pause at the wall before the kitchen. There you hear the landlady and handsome father are having a spitefully hissed argument. He's saying amounts of money, she's saying, No, fuck off I can't. She says, How do you expect me to? A chair moves. Just get out just get out, please go away. He says the words that triangulate something in you, It's my house, Mel.

In the days after the father has left, not a word is spoken about him by the mother or daughter. The motions of the house carry on as if he'd never been there, like nothing could break the soldiering on of crunchy cereal boxes, school bags, bath time, bedtime, the clothes horse, the vacuum. The professor moves out not long after the father left, without saying goodbye, and not a word on that is mentioned either. He'd started coming back late and lurking in his room with the big light on, clearing his throat. You had avoided him for a while, suddenly queasy at his angling for you.

Now it is just you lodging with the mother and child again, the three of you in the morning, but the mood is loose and ambiguous. I'm lost. When is this? The girl has started biting and breaking things. One night for hours she shouts and slams her dolls against the wall until her mother calms her down. Stretched out under freshly cleaned bedding you put headphones on and listen to ocean sound effects until you fall asleep with your mouth open and one hand on your crotch. You wake up to a gnawing orgasm and hear the daughter is crying downstairs. You shower and dress in an outfit Zed designed for you: all in different blues, an erroneous belt, a matching necklace. You blow-dry your hair in careful sections, draw bat wings on your eyes, pack a bag but leave all of your books on the bed before going downstairs. The mother has a bite mark on her arm and is clearing out a drawer full of paperwork, contracts and old bills. You hover behind her. Would you like some coffee? you ask. The mother looks at you helplessly, I'd love coffee ... then adds, You look nice. In the kitchen the little girl is scribbling furiously with a purple crayon on an old letter. She pauses to eat a mouthful of cereal, then starts again, treating it like an important work task; breathing hard, wiping her mouth, pushing her hair back, returning to the scribble. You wish her a happy morning, she ignores you. You kiss her cheek, she squirms and makes a noise, you kiss her other cheek and laugh at her wriggling. Tickle her then tiptoe to the kettle. The house is a nervous stomach but you are moving easily in your heeled shoes, tapping out a difference. Hmmm? you say pulling out the cutlery drawer, He's not in there. Opening the biscuit cupboard, Not in there either. What about here? looking under the sink. She gives in and asks you, laying her spoon to rest, What are you doing? I'm looking for your daddy so I can marry him. She stays quiet until your joke has faded.

Moffa the keys

Without keys I was a stranger under the sky, a casualty of the arbitrariness of locks. My existence model collapsed, dead on the ground. Without a phone or a wallet I was a joke-walker, a lame shopper, a novel outside figure, a disorganised woman with no one to call on and nowhere to go, it was just me and my tiny disaster. Bonkers. Frightening. Fate-aggrieved me. I returned to the train station to ask at the desk but there was no desk, just a sign with a phone number. I walked in a circle around the car park. Vicky? Vicky and I hadn't even exchanged numbers let alone addresses but I knew she was around and I could possibly discover her on a bus again. I couldn't get on a bus. Could I ask a neighbour? God no, not them. Also, my subletter had forbidden me from speaking to the neighbours and I'd signed the contract in agreement. Kav? Where was Kav? Kav was just a cloven, uncooked-rice-drinking monster of my imagination.

The next train arrived and people were walking through the car park. I was in their way wherever I walked. A few of them gave me a look of suspicion and frowned indiscreetly. I sat down on the kerb. It was strange to think about my stuff sitting uselessly in my flat—a bowl of bananas, a stolen umbrella, a toothbrush—awkwardly pointless without me, fatal life-props gearing up for a more successful person to follow in their use. What did I truly have in this moment? An unnecessarily gift-wrapped sleeping tonic, new shoes and the outfit I was wearing. The heavy black pilling jumper.

A plan emerged from the fading mental image of my things: perhaps if I just walked slowly and openly through the streets, with my heart and eyes unobstructed to the world, I would bump into someone who could help. After everything I still believed that if you transmit both need and warmth into the universe, the universe will send something back. Despite this being hardly a plan at all it was realised with immediate success. I set off down a quiet road adjacent to the high street, passed a small church, passed a nursery, passed a working men's club, passed a vet, passed a house that revolted me, passed a house that made me envious of families, passed a house that made me aspirational, stepped over the root of a tree that was breaking the pavement, then bumped into Madden and Lloyd. Madden was smoking and Lloyd was scrubbing his gate. They were both concerned in the way they looked at me. Madden cocked his head, You look quite lost, love, he said, Need some help? Something fundamental about men struck me in that instant: they are the inevitable figures of conclusions. Absolutely fine, thank you, I said, How are you? He sort of laughed and said, Sorry you just looked a little worried. I breathed out No and smiled a workplace smile. So you're all right? O yes. She back yet? Not sure, it's obviously very serious. He scratched his head, Right ... I thought she was away at Bee's. I smiled even more professionally and indicated that I was meant to be walking on. He moved aside and said, I'll let you go. Do let me know if you need anything while she's away. Anything at all. I'm in the workshop most days ... He carried on saying something about his workshop and his timetable, but I had already murmured Thank you, see you later, and walked away from them. Next Monday quiz night, don't forget! Madden called after me. I quickened to a run.

It got cold and windy, and the sun was setting. My fingers went a strange yellow colour and felt numb. Without meaning to I had walked a five-mile loop, its last instalment cut through a park to the back of Moffa's house via the ginnel of back gates. I unhooked Moffa's gate and walked into her small garden with the ease of having done it a million times before. I was there. Her back door was locked but I tried it anyway. I didn't have the key any more. Through the small kitchen window I could see that a single lamp was on. Did I leave it on? Has she been back?

It was strange in Moffa's garden, I didn't feel as locked out from her house as I did from my sublet. Why? The yard area was comforting. The amount of pot plants and furniture crammed into the six-by-eight-foot space made the outside feel like inside, where the outside was an attitudinal mess and the inside was the same but slightly warmer. A crow ornament guarded a tomato plant, an overgrowing buddleia sheltered some rotting Sunday supplements, some solar-powered lanterns were spotted with birdshit. So much stuff: my body merged with it all. My body was after all also one of her projects in undignifying nature. I plucked an apple from a branch leaning over from the neighbour's side and sat on a swinging hammock chair to bite and slurp it. It was delicious. I eased back and took out the bottle of sleep aid, dropping twice the directed amount onto my tongue. Then I gave in to the quick calm of evening birdsong, to the relief of overgrownness in the shelter of outside made safe by the resourcefulness of an eccentric. Bless Moffa's state of mind as a garden. Dusk fell and solar light sticks dotted around the patio began to glow. A plastic trickling water feature buzzed ambitiously. There was no need to think any more. No need to worry or miss anyone. I had everything I needed and enough comfort to close my eyes, use my jacket as a blanket and sway in the hammock on the patio. Bless Moffa's garden as somewhere to sit, to forget, to be one of the creatures that sleeps.

* * *

The sky went a nuclear peach colour. All garden life was pulsing and gasping. Gaseous vegetal trailers and pink-lipped flowers with dark, musky herbs, nightmare-winged little birds dipping towards the light, drips from the leaking water feature, drain smell—I was part of it all.

The top of a man's head was suddenly hovering above the gate. Half-asleep and short of senses, I half-understood what it was. But soon the man's head took on significance so I pulled myself together quietly and said, Hello? My heart beating like a rabbit. Whoever it was opened the gate and came into the garden. He was familiar in a way, not very tall, calm-postured with confident, quick movements. He was looking around the garden for something, me, the person who had said, Hello? I was camouflaged among all the things that dangled in Moffa's garden. He couldn't see me. I was terrified and wished I hadn't spoken. He stood by a dying lobelia. He saw me. I sat silent and stunned, partially excited, unable to speak. I have this for you, he said in a familiar warm voice. He held up my bag. I understood. My bag. That's my bag. He carried on holding it up. It's taken me hours to find you, how about some breakfast? I gently tipped myself out of the hammock and walked over to receive my bag from the man who didn't scare me any more. He was my age. His clothes were messy but he wore them with a smartness. I was instantly attracted to him. The fabric of the shirt he wore was a nice quality, with a modish round collar.

O no, my keys? I said. He smiled at me. His smile made me blush. My keys aren't in here. I looked up at him like he could straightforwardly answer this. He smiled more, like I was sweet and stupid, and said, I don't know about your keys. We both peered into the bag. All that was in there was a child's toy and a pair of lace knickers. His hair was greasy and falling forward and nearly touched mine. I wanted him to hold my hand. Thank you, I said, but worried about my keys. For some reason I leaned on him. Are you locked out? he said, I can help. Yes I am, but not from here. I live in a block just over there, around the corner. It's a sublet. Do you love me? He looked at Moffa's back door without answering. I don't live here, I said. The man was standing on some flowers. He really smiled at me, Well, I can help you get in anywhere you want. What for? I asked. He didn't answer, just took a small leather-bound toolkit out of his pocket and laid it on the floor. Let's sit down for a bit first. I'm knackered. He pulled out a deckchair and unfolded it, wiping away leaves and dirt, half whistling, half singing a song about a girl who ran away. Are you Vicky's dad? I asked, and I didn't know why. I don't know Vicky, he said, then, Have you got anything to eat? Now his legs were wide and relaxed, he looked crueler. All the berries and apples are gone. He sighed an exaggerated sigh then said, You've grown so gorgeous. What? I don't know you. But I wanted him to say it again. There was silence for a moment, just the creak of the fence. Then he did say it again, You've grown so, so gorgeous. He closed his eyes and continued saying it, You've really grown, slowly and with his breath, You've grown so gorgeously, he said, as if the phrase brought him gratification just to say it, he was pleasuring himself with this complex comment on me, subtly grinding into the cloth seat as he repeated it. The morning sun had come around and lit him. There must be some food, he said. I shook my head. His next words shocked me, She usually has some pizzas in the freezer. He walked over to the back door and pulled it violently towards him. It rattled in its frame almost worriedly. How do you know that? Have you been here before? O yeah. He started banging on the door furiously. Here, I passed him his tools. He took them and kicked the door, then said, Or stew, she sometimes has a stew. I didn't believe Moffa had a stew. I didn't like the way he kicked the door. Every small screwdriver and pin he used made a screeching sound, so high-pitched I had to back away. Hang on, I'm not ready, I said. He stopped and looked at me, You're right, we can't go in there yet. He turned around and started kicking the plant pots, knocking them over and smashing them, then kicking around the dislodged flowers, stamping on the perennials. I sat back on the hammock. He was laughing a little. And then he vomited onto his tools and had to fish out a small screwdriver from the pool of sick, then he carried on working the lock, quietly and calmly. The screeching sound continued.

Nearly got it, he said, Got it. There was a breaking sound and I woke up. I was shivering in the hammock, alone in the garden without my bag. It was still light, or maybe it was light again. A voice called, Hello?

You arrive

On an insultingly sunny morning a removal van will arrive and the mother and child will have to leave the house. Who knows where they will go, what they can do. He who owns the house broke a promise, arrived with debt, demanded rent, decided to move in. He will paint the walls a greyish white. He'll bring gym equipment and tools, new young pets, a record collection. The clear sky above the house is dazzling with ownership, its slow, clean curse. The birds scream and find each other.

There is a bag of things: the girl's favourite doll that was found in the garden, some old jewellery, an accounting book. You are jolly and polite to the grandmother as you pass the bag to her at the door. She takes them from you and says, Well look at you, he's a liar, and you're a stupid little tart. You wince at the words and seem confused that she doesn't like you, you're simply happy, everyone's had a nice time. She'll grow to accept it, you think, and the little girl can come to visit any time. A new promise has been made, one that sees you slip easily back onto the garden furniture. You sigh as the taxi with the grandmother in it pulls away. You are hot from the sun and you love it because you came here, you arrived. You have everything now: a place to be touched in and determined by. You'll go, It's in my bedroom, my well-being parlour, lalala, I'll see my clients here, my love, Where's my kitchen, What's in my garden. He'll laugh, you'll sign your name, lalala.

Moffa the clock

Hello, are you all right? the voice called again.

Moffa's voice. It was her extravagant curdling vocals, her elongated, sing-song Hello, full of faithful up notes. Because, did you know, Hello is always a question? Hello asks, Are you there? Are you someone I can communicate with? Are you in need of help or are you able to offer help? Sing Hello back, admit we are fog. Hello was all that I needed to hear. I was awake.

Hello? I asked back.

Hang on, I can't hear you very well. Moffa's voice was loud and real, was mine?

I'm here! I waved from the hammock. Even from within my own head my voice sounded quiet and useless, an echo looking for a surface; Moffa's an oar slicing through water.

O right, yes that's better. I can hear you now. No, it's me. It's me!

Let me just find a key and open the back door.

Yes please. I'm locked out.

The key jangled and the back door swished into the fence but Moffa was hidden behind a plant. Her red shoes walked back inside. She was still talking in long, tuneful sentences. I stood up and walked towards the door, ducking under a vine.

Did you have a lovely time? I whispered towards the house.

I had a wonderful time, she called, Hills and views, she said, I von-Trapped the joint, drank loads, o poor tomatoes.

How are you? How's the motor?

I don't know what you mean.

My legs ached from being curled up in the hammock all night. Or was it just an hour? Was this evening light or morning? I shuffled up to the door at the exact time Moffa stepped out of it with an overfull watering can in her hand. She halted, nearly bashing into me, just like when I was a child. Her gardening arm muscles protruded through chiffon. Water sploshed onto my feet, it was real. She looked at me in horror. In her other hand she held her phone to her ear. She was on the phone.

Is it possible for the answer to Hello to be No? No, it is not me, I'm not the one you're talking to. This is a fog that found a shape. Keep talking.

Moffa naturally, almost miraculously, unfroze and reformed herself, her attention only to the phone and whomever was on it. She stepped around me to water her plants. O you're joking, what a rascal, love him, ah my poor tomatoes, all shrivelled, I missed the last of them, and what did he say? She neatened the hammock and picked up my jacket, and without looking at me, handed it over, I was shivering. Then in much the same gesture as she shifted me to the side, Moffa picked dead leaves off the floor and inspected a bush ... No ... yes ... mine need pruning. She lifted and replaced the watering can while I hovered behind her in my jacket. Once the can was empty she strode back inside, leaving the door open. The kettle clunked against the tap, it clicked on, moaned into action. I went inside. Hahahahah (actor laugh), no, no, you're being silly ... hahahaha ... What? ... Yes ... I sat down on the tiny stool in the kitchen and watched Moffa put tea bags in two cups. She's here now actually. Right here, yes ... O who knows ...

A cup of tea was handed to me. Then a large warm hand was placed flat on top of my head ... Very cold ... Silly ... What? O she's OK. He did, yes, he messaged ... More movements around the kitchen, opening, wiping, screwing and unscrewing lids ... O it's a lovely flat. Sweet boys. I know, so sad ... Well he's not using it is he? I tell you what ...

Perhaps I was tired after all. Perhaps I just needed to remember what a house felt like: kettle noises and taps turning; talking on the phone; sunshine through the window. I looked at the clock above the sink that was a silhouette of Charlie Chaplin. His cane said 7:36. The evening. Thank God. How nice.

... It's just around the corner, she can have it for as long as she needs. Well, they owe me, after last Halloween. I don't like lying, I don't mind lying to the police but not when I'm retrograding hahahaha (actor laugh)!

I sipped my tea and observed the Charlie Chaplin clock. His little cane flicked minute into minute. So funny. Minute, a minute more, like clicks of a door, shift, shift, edge to the end. Hello, having a mad time? Dead good weather? Can I live with you? Tick. Tick.

I burped. Moffa looked at me and scowled. She carried on talking to whomever was on the phone about some nice boys who lived in a flat nearby. The cup was empty except for some golden sludge of sugar so I put it in the sink, stepped back out into the garden, weaved through the plants, out the back gate, along the path, up the road. Damn the lot, I said, No more good life badly done or good life ruined. Why not once and for all just climb inside the sandwich box?

They say that the ideal place to live is halfway up a hill. At that level you can relax without getting stuck. Towns that are low down, at canal or lake level, hold you under. Too high up and you feel you might blow away or become a cloud. Villages are full of people too wind-battered or too sunken; people who can't concentrate for moving and people who can't move at all. This town is the perfect distance up from water. I'll tell her how nice her garden is looking and that I'm just round the corner if she needs me. I'm going to work in a well-being shop and can get anything she needs for her well-being. Then I'll rub people like birds.

The boy with the football was returning just ahead of me, he held the front door of the block open as I strode through. I smelt his deodorant. I arrived at my door and simply knocked. The door opened. Kav had a young smile. Kav was frying onions, making the flat smell delicious and drinking a glass of Coke. The chorus of my kind of song was coming from a small speaker on the counter.

You're back? The music soared. You're frying onions!

You're home!

You're so funny.

Acknowledgements

The name 'Moffa' was co-invented with Emma Bennett during an improvised performance for Camarade at the Arnolfini Art Centre, 2013.

'I will be glad when this is over' (p. 89) recalls a line from 'Bog-Face' by Stevie Smith, found in *Collected Poems and Drawings of Stevie Smith* (London: Faber, 2015).

Vicky's school-gate impression is based on a scene from the British sitcom *Bottom* ('Contest,' BBC, 1 October, 1991).

I am grateful to Joanna Lee and Caitlin Leydon for their special intervention, to early readers Rachel Genn and Emma Bennett, to Karolina Sutton and Anne Meadows, to Lucy Luck, to Rachael Allen ever so, to my mother for the thing about pickled onions in lemonade, and to Luke Kennard.

PHOTO CREDIT: ELEANOR VONNE BROWN

Holly Pester is a poet, novelist, and academic based in Essex, UK. She has worked in sound art and performance, with original dramatic work on BBC Radio 4, and collaborations with the Serpentine Galleries, Women's Art Library and Wellcome Collection. Her poetry has been published extensively. *Comic Timing*, her collection of poetry, was published by Granta in 2021.

Printed by Imprimerie Gauvin
Gatineau, Québec